Ghosts
of
Nova Scotia

Darryll Walsh

Pottersfield Press, Lawrencetown Beach, Nova Scotia, Canada

Canadian Cataloguing in Publication Data

Walsh, Darryll

    Ghosts of Nova Scotia

    ISBN 1-395900-31-X

1. Ghosts — Nova Scotia — History.   I. Title.
GR113.5N69W35 2000   398.2'09716'05   C00-950128-2

Cover design: Gail LeBlanc, at Dal Graphics

Pottersfield Press gratefully acknowledges the ongoing support of the Nova Scotia Department of Tourism and Culture, Cultural Affairs Division, as well as The Canada Council for the Arts. We acknowledge the financial support of the Government of Canada through the Book Publishing Industry Development Program for our publishing activities.

Printed in Canada

Pottersfield Press
83 Leslie Road
East Lawrencetown
Nova Scotia, Canada, B2Z 1P8

To order, telephone free of charge 1-800-NIMBUS9 (1-800-646-2879)

For Absent Friends . . .
They are worthy of everlasting love and remembrance,
until the morning breaks
and we meet again

Je me souviens

and

For Lost Loves
which haunt me still . . .

Table of Contents

Acknowledgements

No book is the result of a single person. For this one I have been helped and encouraged by many people, only a few of whom I can thank here.

For their love and understanding I must first thank my parents. I can never repay the debt I owe.

I wish to thank the patrons, staff and executive of the Halifax Regional Police Association, both past and present, for their support and understanding through both births of this book. Their faith kept me going.

A special thank you has to go out to Cheryl Yates, who graciously resurrected the manuscript that was all that I had left after the computer disk crashed. Through her patience and editing, I was able to recreate this work.

A very large thank you goes to my editors, who painfully waded through the rough drafts, as well as my publisher, Lesley Choyce, and all who contributed to the final product.

Another special thanks goes to Mary-Anne Hopkins, who was very helpful in procuring the pictures used in this book.

I would like to thank Dr. Mark Goisine, who owns the Robie Street Palace and was kind enough to send me all the information he had on the house so that I was able to understand the true nature of the haunting.

Also I wish to thank Valerie Inness from the Queens County Museum for her help in sending me authenticating information on various stories.

And now a blanket thank you and acknowledgement of the faith and excitement that many expressed upon hearing this project.

Introduction

Some of the locations and stories here are smothered both in the figurative and literal mists of time. But that is part of the eerie nature of tracking hauntings. Many of the stories are so old as to be almost lost to us through these mists, while others, we might wish they were. Some of the stories are the kind you could hear anywhere, while others are decidedly British or French. Still more have that unique Nova Scotian flavour to them.

Nova Scotia has a heritage deeply connected to the sea, so it should not come as a surprise to learn that many of the stories found here are related to the sea. This includes one of the most disturbing mysteries of all time, the disappearance of the *Mary Celeste*. The sea casts its spell upon the land through the fog that creeps in after supper, and only reluctantly loosens its grip come the light of morning. With it may come a chill that moves down your spine and into your heart as you freeze at suddenly amplified sounds, muffled sounds, or worse . . . no sound at all. You can't see where you're going, nor the person next to you, but you know something is with you. All around you. Perhaps it is the presence of a ghost documented in this book.

It is entertaining to be able to look upon ghastly things from a safe distance. That is why I wrote this book. I have catalogued more than 140 stories and mysterious places for you to visit in order to bring the eeriness and horror of some of our favourite fears just a little bit closer. This book is not intended as a comprehensive discussion of every ghost or haunting in the province; instead, it serves as a guide for you to discover for yourself the places where something strange has happened. And may happen again. Everything from ghosts to poltergeists to mermaids, could walk with you along a lonely road in the middle of nowhere, with only the muffled whispers of the gloom to lead the way. Also included are tales of buried treasure since they are so often associated with ghost appearances.

Why do we like these stories so much? They feed a perpetual need to be both excited and scared, albeit in a safe venue. I certainly have loved such stories ever since I was a child. About once a week my Aunt Phyllis and Uncle Basil would come over to visit my parents. They would talk about ordinary things for the first hour or so, and then I would be sent to bed. However, I always knew that shortly after the hour was up, some exceptional stories would be told, so I crept out of bed and huddled by the door. Most I have forgotten, but one or two still cling to me like the damp mist of our fog-shrouded province.

My mother's family is from River Bourgeois in Richmond County, Cape Breton. One of the first stories I heard about the old homestead concerned one of my uncles who was fighting in World War II. For a few days before my Uncle Augustaine was killed in Holland, the rocking chair in the kitchen would rock on its own with no one near. After my uncle's death, it ceased its mysterious rocking and never did it again. This would be a case of a classic forerunner, and the story was one of the reasons I grew to love the paranormal. This tale would be retold from time to time if there were new people visiting and so, many nights, I drifted off to sleep with visions of that rocking chair in my head.

It wouldn't have been possible to complete this book if it wasn't for the groundwork that was laid by other authors in this genre. Helen Creighton, Edith Mosher, Roland Sherwood, Thomas Raddall, and others, have all contributed both to our knowledge of the folklore and customs of Nova Scotia and to this book. It was not possible for me to track each and every story in this book, so I relied on the excellent work already done and now I present it in this unique format. Many of these stories occurred long ago and the principal characters are now dead or have moved on. Nevertheless, the stories have outlived them and continue to fascinate and titillate us.

I couldn't include every scary story or strange custom, for it would be impossible to pin them all down. No book can be totally inclusive. There will always be new stories or different versions to tell. As well, the prime characteristic of every story had to be its accessibility. I hope the book will serve as an unique portrait of Nova Scotia. For this, I had to be reasonably sure of where each incident was located both in space and time. Therefore, some of my personal favourites, and perhaps some of the readers', are missing. For this I apologize. But I hope that I have included enough known and new locations to give the reader an exciting view of the province. To protect the privacy of present occupants, I have occasionally been vague and suggested that you ask politely of those in the area about a location. That way I am not sending hundreds of people to someone's door enquiring about their ghost or other skeletons in the closet.

We all have our favourite eerie story of something that has happened to us. You know, the one we confide to our friends in a whisper when we get together over our favourite beverage, and sometimes only in that condition. Sometimes it only takes a stormy night with the right atmosphere and a need to validate the experience. As the catchphrase for Dean Koontz's book *Whispers* goes, "Fear shouts, terror whispers!"

Once I awoke and reflexively looked down at the foot of my bed. Sitting there were two small black demons with piercing red eyes. No hair, nor ears, just a shiny black coating of skin. And those awful piercing red eyes. When my head came up to confirm what it was I was seeing, they turned to look at me, then dropped to the floor. I was outside my room and halfway down the stairs before my rational self managed to regain control. It was a long time that I spent standing on the stairs in the middle of the night, listening for any sound from my room. Eventually, I gathered the nerve to go back upstairs, and upon turning on the light, reassured myself that all was well, and that it had only been a dream. But I didn't check under the bed.

In psychology and sleep research we might call this experience an example of creating a hypnopompic state. It might have taken the form of an after-image of a dream, one that continues for a few seconds into waking reality. Although my training tells me the after-images came from the dream, my heart tells me otherwise, for I wasn't dreaming of them before I awoke.

Maybe those demons were after-images. Maybe it was a product of the chocolate cake I had eaten before bed. Maybe the images were a dream from one of the books by Stephen King I was reading at the time. Or maybe there are other explanations that can be quite unsettling.

So make yourself comfortable as I stoke up the fire. It's cold and damp out tonight, and the fog's coming in. And there are some stories that must be told.

Cumberland County

Fort Beausejour National Park, Nova Scotia/New Brunswick border

This was the former Acadian fort, rebuilt into a national shrine. When the Acadians were expelled, many apparently left behind valuables, buried for an eventual return. Most never did return, and this treasure still remains to this day. Over the years stories have been told of poor farmers suddenly coming into money, strange signs of digging in the night and ghostly apparitions still guarding the treasure. Practically anywhere in this area could hold a fortune, just a short distance beneath your feet. From here you can see the Tantramar Marshes.

Tantramar Marshes

These flatlands with the Missaquash River flowing through them were at one time land belonging to the Acadians. Before they were deported, some were said to have buried their valuables with the idea of returning to claim them in the future. Over the years these small caches grew into stores of great buried treasure, and there is anecdotal evidence that some people have found something of value buried throughout these marshes.

A French girl and her lover, a British soldier, came to a sad end here. They were captured by the local Mi'kmaq tribe who were angry over the deaths of some of their members at the hands of the British. The Mi'kmaq planned an especially torturous end for the young lovers. When the tide was out on the Missaquash River they tied the soldier and his lady love to stakes in the red clay that formed the banks of the river. They tied the soldier to a stake nearer the water, so that when the inevitable return of the tide occurred, she would watch her lover drown before she would meet her own end. After the waters had risen and drowned the soldier, troops arrived to save the young girl. But, legend has it, she had no desire to remain on this earth without her true love, so she lowered her head and allowed the waters to take her to join her lover in death. To this day it is said that their ghosts can be seen by the river when the tide rushes in and if you listen carefully, the gurgling waters sound like two people drowning.

Somewhere along the river, close to Fort Lawrence, there was a road with a bridge that was the scene of bloody fighting between the British and the Mi'kmaq. It was renamed Bloody Bridge, but locals said that the cries of battle and the dying could still be heard, so the road was moved and the bridge destroyed. If you like wandering cold and lonely places, take a walk around here after you visit the fort, and you may hear the sounds of battle and the cries of the dead.

Finally, from here there is the story of the ghost of an Acadian girl, who still walks the marshes with a lantern looking for her lover who was expelled with the rest of the Acadians.

Jollicure

Of all the supposed buried treasure in this area the largest and most valuable is said to be buried here. One day early in the nineteenth century, a local farmer had to rescue his cow from a sinkhole on his property. Upon closer inspection, he saw that the sinkhole was in fact a man-made pit that had collapsed. The pit was found to be twenty-five feet in diameter and had workings similar to that of the infamous Money Pit of Oak Island, discussed later in this book.

As with the Money Pit, there were regular wooden platforms at ten foot intervals, except these were said to have mysterious markings which were destroyed by the farmer and his cohorts. Perhaps if they had taken the time to read or save the markings, they might have solved this puzzle. But like those at the Money Pit for the last two hundred years, they tried to find the treasure through brute strength alone. Well, nature and/or the original diggers had a surprise for them. Just after the thirty foot level, a great torrent of water rushed in and all attempts at bailing were unsuccessful. Though drilling and an auger produced evidence that there was gold and silver buried far below, no one has been able to get to it. Perhaps if they hadn't destroyed the markings on the first platform, they might have had the instructions on how to overcome the water.

Amherst

Coming from Amherst is one of the most documented and strangest occurrences of ghostly phenomena. Poltergeists, ghostly voices and spirit writing all revolved around Esther Cox in the nineteenth century.

The location of the Great Amherst Mystery was at 6 Princess Street in Amherst. The house is no longer there, having been replaced by a Canadian Tire store. Back in 1878 and '79 the house belonged to a Daniel Teed and his wife Olive. Staying with the Teeds were their two children, Olive's brother William and two sisters, Jane and Ester, and Daniel's brother John. Esther was eighteen years old that September 4 when the first of the mysterious happenings began.

One week before Esther had broken up with her boyfriend, who threatened her by waving a pistol in her face. Needless to say, this wasn't conducive to a life-long match, nor to a calm mind for some time afterwards. No matter what her state of mind, Esther was sleeping peacefully in the bed she and her sister shared. She awoke to the sounds of something moving under the bed. She woke up Jane, they investigated and found that a box under the bed was jumping up and down as if some animal were inside. They called Daniel Teed, and when he opened the box he found nothing in it to make it act as it had. Everyone returned to bed and the rest of the night passed peacefully.

The next night was interrupted by Esther screaming out, "I'm dying." When everyone rushed into the bedroom and lit some candles, they saw Esther's body was badly swollen as she cried out in pain. More sounds were coming from under the bed, but before anyone could investigate, a loud clap of thunder was heard in the room. Immediately Esther fell back to sleep and her body returned to a normal state.

From then on classic poltergeist activity began. Bedclothes would be pulled off beds by unseen hands, whispers would be heard, and objects moved apparently by themselves. The local doctor was called and examined Esther, but could not find anything wrong with her. It was at this time that writing appeared on her bedroom wall. "Esther Cox, you are mine to kill," was written by a ghostly hand in front of a half-dozen witnesses.

Soon knocks and raps began on the walls and ceilings. Someone began to speak to the unseen presence and it answered questions with knocks. Naturally the story soon got out and villagers flocked to the house to see for themselves the fascinating phenomena. Even the local Methodist preacher observed a pail of water start to boil when it was placed near Esther.

Esther became sick with diphtheria, and for the two-week duration of her illness no bizarre happenings occurred. She was also sent to stay with relatives for a time. Upon her return she was given a new room in the house, with the hope that a change of location would continue to exorcise the ghost. It was all for naught, however. Soon fires began to drop from the ceilings and after a few days of this, Esther was banned from the house.

Esther found a job and room with a local restaurant owner, but the problem followed her there so the poor girl was quickly returned to the Teed residence. She was then shipped off to Saint John, New Brunswick, to be studied but none of the phenomena followed her there, so she returned to Amherst. A local farmer then had the grace to offer her a place to stay and while there she lived a happy, quiet life. However, when Olive Teed intervened to have her sister returned to the Teed house, the phenomena returned with her and at an increased rate.

An American actor and magician, Walter Hubbell then entered the picture. He stayed with Esther for five weeks and observed all that occurred around her, including knives that were sent through the air at him. This gave him the idea to take Esther on the stage circuit. They arranged a show but it flopped miserably. Not totally discouraged at this turn of events, Hubbell wrote a book on the incident called *The Great Amherst Mystery*.

Esther meanwhile was employed by another local farmer until his barn burnt down and she was arrested for arson and jailed for three months. After that, and until her death in 1912, Esther Cox was free of any further incidents.

Many parapsychologists have thought long and hard on this series of events. The predominant theory is that the phenomena was triggered by the trauma of the near rape at the hands of her boyfriend, the week previous to the first event. Poltergeists are believed to be the product of a stressed and/or sexually frustrated mind, usually a female adolescent. If Esther was suffering trauma from the boyfriend incident, coupled with a theory that Daniel Teed may have been "bothering" her, the events might be explained by using the "unconscious psychokinesis" theory of poltergeists. Nevertheless, no one has been able to develop a better theory or to debunk this series of bizarre events.

Spencer's Island

Spencer's Island is well known as one of the two best ship building areas of Nova Scotia. Lunenburg serviced the Atlantic side of the province, while Spencer's Island served the Fundy Shore. It is from here that one of the most well-known mysteries of our time began. Ship building was the forte of the people there, but it is one ship in particular that Spencer's Island is famous for.

She was built and named the *Amazon* in May 1861, and was a brigantine of 282 tons. She was only 103 feet long, but her legend dwarfs many a ship of larger dimensions. Most know her as the *Mary Celeste*.

In November 1872, she left New York harbour, bound for Genoa, Italy. At the same time, the British ship *Del Gratia* left New York for Gibralter. On December 4, the *Del Gratia*, having just come out of a squall, came upon the *Mary Celeste* sailing erratically. Captain Morehouse of the *Del Gratia* became concerned and sent a boarding party over to examine the ship. However, upon boarding the ship, the search party found her to be totally deserted, and no reason for her abandonment could be determined. *Mary Celeste* was in pretty good order, although there were small tears in her sails. Her cargo of alcohol was still there and many valuables were untouched. A hatch was open, with some water in the hold, but no-

21

where near enough to have required the crew to abandon ship.

Captain Morehouse sent a crew over to the *Mary Celeste* to take her into Gibralter. Once there, the legal niceties of salvage dragged on for some time as theories as to what happened developed and, during this century, grew stranger.

Various theories have been put forward for the strange disappearance of Captain Briggs, his wife, their daughter, and the crew of the *Mary Celeste*. Everything from the Bermuda Triangle, to UFOs, to the *Del Gratia* crew becoming pirates and seizing the ship. This last theory was partially to blame for the long delay in awarding the *Del Gratia* salvage money. And, as it turned out, not very much money.

The most likely explanation to the long-standing mystery is that the captain and crew became wary after some of the cargo of alcohol started leaking in the hold. Alcohol fumes are quite flammable and it was possible that the crew thought the ship was in mortal danger. They may have taken to the ship's boat and run a line to the ship, but a squall may have developed and the line may have been broken. A small lifeboat would not last long in the Atlantic and the captain and crew, along with his wife and daughter, would have drowned. The *Mary Celeste*, meanwhile, would have continued on her way only to be spotted by the *Del Gratia* and the mystery was born. However, exactly what happened on the *Mary Celeste* that day and the fate of her crew will remain a mystery forever.

Parrsboro

There are two haunted bridges in Parrsboro. At Lank's Bridge an apparition of a horse with a headless rider can be seen, apparently the result of a murder many years ago.

At Frog Hollow Bridge the ghost of a young girl is seen and the sounds of her screams can be heard as well. She perished here one cold Halloween night.

Black Point

It was the year 1740, and the seas were a dangerous place for some. Many blood-thirsty pirates still sailed these waters, as well as warships because of the continuing war between Britain and France.

One of the ships that sailed these waters was called the *Red Hawk*, captained by Jonathan Hawkins. During what was to be the last voyage of the *Red Hawk*, Captain Hawkins had with him his daughter Elizabeth, as her mother had passed away some years earlier. But this voyage was no place for Elizabeth. They were overtaken by the savage pirate Lenardo Dano, captain of the *Diavola*, who slaughtered all but Captain Hawkins and six of his sailors. Earlier Hawkins had thrown his daughter overboard in order to save her, but the pirates saw what the captain had done and had launched a boat to rescue her just before the battle began. The six survivors of the crew walked the plank; Hawkins was next and the last sight he saw was that of his daughter being held by the pirates.

A hurricane picked that fortunate time to come up and Elizabeth was spared for a time. The *Diavola* weathered the storm and landed near Black Point. Legend has it the pirates saw jewels and precious stones washed ashore and filled the ship full of them. Meanwhile, Eliza-

beth had spit in Dano's face and scratched him, so he decided to punish her with a cruel death. He found a cave
not far from the shore and throwing Elizabeth in it, with
only some fish, he ordered it sealed.

Many years later some Mi'kmaq were investigating
the area and one of them entered the cave. He found the
cave rich in amethyst and quartz, but he also found a
skeleton. From this cave, known as the "Maiden's Cave,"
have been heard through the years the anguished, ghostly
cries of the girl who was sealed alive by the pirate she
spurned.

Colchester County

Five Islands

Of these five islands, Long Island is the supposed resting place of treasure buried by Spanish sailors. Long Island is the central island and in the centre of it there are three graves, with the middle one hiding Spanish doubloons underneath. A local man had purchased a pirate map from a down-on-his-luck sailor. He led a few men on a treasure hunt, but death and misadventure claimed one of them and was in danger of claiming them all before they were rescued. The local man disappeared after that, leading some to believe he had found something. But he couldn't have taken it all. Are there still some hidden doubloons under the third grave on Long Island?

Also on Long Island is the angry spirit of an evil man who was murdered by his sons. He cries out for vengeance while roaming the island. It is said his face is embedded on a rock called Buff's Ghost.

Hants County

Maitland

MacCallum House in Maitland was built by a ship-builder in the early 1700s. It has operated as a Bed and Breakfast and it appears to have had more than its share of guests. Local legend has it that Archie MacCallum murdered a slave and buried him next to the well. The restless spirit of the slave now haunts the premises and other apparitions have been seen in the windows.

Nearby is Lawrence House, whose builder dearly loved violin music. Some say his music can still be heard from the house. Other strange noises come from the basement.

There is still another haunted house in the general area. Springhurst House is haunted by a knocking on the doors and a voice calling out "Lou."

Moosebrook

Laffin House is haunted by two spirits. One walks the halls, while another has opened doors and lifted mirrors off the wall.

Windsor

Windsor is the location of the home of Thomas Chandler Haliburton, nineteenth-century judge and author of the Sam Slick stories. It is now a museum but some say the spirit of Haliburton still calls it home. The judge's ghost is said to emerge from a secret panel in the wall of the reception hall and wander about for awhile before disappearing through the same section of wall. If you visit, keep a sharp eye when in the reception hall.

Also on the grounds of Haliburton House is the ghostly vision of a kilted soldier of the Black Watch regiment, who is said to have drowned in a pond as he and his fellow soldiers marched through the forty-acre estate. The pool is called the "Piper's Pond" because the unfortunate soldier was the regiment's piper. Local legend has it that if you should run around the pond twenty times, the soldier will come up out of the black depths on the back of a horse.

At Kings College, a private school, the apparition of the old headmaster, Pa Buckle, still walks the halls as he did in former times. After he retired from teaching the school allowed him to stay on the premises, so I guess he just assumed that the invitation was still open after his death. He was seen walking the grounds in formal dress from time to time. The College burnt down in 1920, but the legend still lives.

There are also sightings in Windsor of a lonely apparition of a woman who walks along the shore of the Avon River before a storm.

Mount Uniacke

Stately Uniacke House, home of Richard John Uniacke, attorney general of Nova Scotia in the early 1800s, boasts two ghosts: a mother and a daughter. Staff are unsure why the wife and daughter of Uniacke have decided to remain earthbound here, but perhaps it is due to their love of this quiet estate which is now a museum. The ghosts of Martha Uniacke and her eldest daughter, Lady Mary Mitchell, are said to be seen walking arm in arm along the lake on the estate, or sitting quietly inside the house. Lady Mitchell is usually at the piano and her mother is sitting close by. Staff and visitors alike have seen the pair or sensed their presence, so a trip to Uniacke House is well the worth the time for those who are daring and may wish to encounter a pair of restless spirits.

Kings County

Wolfville

Wolfville is one of the prettier towns in the Annapolis Valley, and it is the location of Acadia University. Here at Acadia there is a resident ghost. In the women's residence is the ghost of a blond woman which has been seen haunting the Prophet's Room. The Prophet's Room is a suite that was built with the residence in 1879, and it is in this room that sightings have occurred of a woman calmly combing her long blond hair. No one is sure of the ghost's supposed identity.

Cape Blomidon

It is here, Mi'kmaq legends say, the great Glooscap resides.

Lately there has been scholarly speculation that Glooscap may actually have been Prince Henry Sinclair, Earl of Orkney, from Scotland, who is believed to have sailed to Nova Scotia in 1398. There are some similarities between Glooscap and Henry Sinclair suggestive of a connection.

There are also stories of a mysterious light that can be seen flashing from Cape Blomidon, which locals call the Eye of Glooscap. There are some who believe it to be light reflecting off a huge amethyst, but no one has found it yet.

Kentville

A local inn here boasts the ghost of an artist. The artist hanged himself because of a woman and since then there have been noises in one of the rooms. In one case, he appeared and stayed the night with a guest. A polite question to a local person may elicit the inn's name.

Berwick

In 1967 there were reports of an eighteen-foot Big Foot-like creature roaming the area. Whereas there is a strong possibility that there are unclassified hominids roaming the Pacific Northwest of the U.S. and Canada, the possibility of one, especially one of eighteen feet, roaming these parts is slightly less plausible.

Hall's Harbour

During the War of 1812, privateers would often put in to small harbours for provisions, for safety, or for companionship. In 1813 Captain Samuel Hall was making a fair booty plundering the American coast during the War of 1812. He was also in the habit of plundering a small village nine miles from Kentville. The settlers of the town didn't take very kindly to this and on May 30, 1813, they planned an ambush for the captain. Captain Hall managed to get away, however, but he lost his treasure when the settlers ambushed a member of his crew who was attempting to hide it. The blood of the now dead pirate scared the settlers and they buried the treasure themselves. Superstition kept them away from the site for some time and eventually they forgot the final resting place of the fortune. To this day there are those who seek the considerable treasure buried somewhere along the shore.

Also seen every seven years at Hall's Harbour are the ghostly lights of a ship sailing up the Bay of Fundy.

Annapolis County

Margaretsville

From here comes the story of the mysterious silent lady. She showed up at a house along the shore one evening, looking a little worse for wear, so a family let her in. She would say nothing, though, even when asked her name. The family stayed with her all night, but she remained mute. The next morning, she got up from the chair she had spent the previous twelve hours on and walked off as silently as she had come, never to return.

Annapolis Royal

In the oldest house of the town there are a pair of ghosts that appear from time to time. The Checkered Lady is the most famous. She appears in the rocking chair she died in, wearing the same dress. Also in the house is the ghost of a slave girl who met her end locked up alone in a closet.

Also coming from Annapolis Royal is the story of a ghostly duel. Legend has it that a suitor of a lovely local lady was late one day in meeting his true love. When he finally arrived at her residence, he told a surprising story to her and her family.

Apparently the night before he had stayed at a local inn that is now the location of the Royal Bank. During the night he was awoken by the sounds of someone trying to get into his room. When he got himself half out of the covers, he was frightened by the appearance of two men dressed in clothes from long ago. To add to his fright, the men were armed with long sabers and proceeded to have a duel in his room. The duel finally ended when one man ran the less fortunate one through and then tossed him out the window. Upon this act, the victor winked at the frightened guest.

Apparently the sight of the ghostly duel scared the guest so badly he was too frightened to move for quite some time and this accounted for his lateness at his lady love's place. The woman and her family did not really believe him, yet years later when the inn was torn down to build the present Royal Bank, a skeleton with a saber alongside it was found buried below.

Also at Annapolis Royal is Fort Anne, a British bastion of military authority established to counteract French influence in the region. Today it is a pretty and quiet area, favoured by tourists and locals alike during the day. After dark and late into the night, however, locals who live near Fort Anne can hear the plaintive sound of the Phantom Drummer. No one knows who he was or why he remains, but his presence has been noted by those living near or visiting the fort.

Granville Ferry

Many years ago a young girl was thrown from her horse and killed. Now it is said every seven years you can hear the horse galloping up the road, but it is never seen.

Also at Granville Ferry, in an old Victorian house named The Moorings, the ghost of a former owner still walks her house. The ghost seems to be active whenever there are changes made to the house.

Stony Beach

The Grey Lady of Stony Beach walks the shore here, her name coming from the drab colour of her last set of clothes on this earth. It is said that she was murdered and, if you are brave enough to ask her, she will tell you her murderer.

Victoria Beach

Along the cliffs of Victoria Beach you can see the ghost of a woman who committed suicide. One difference between her and other ghostly wanderers is that she is clearly seen wearing an apron.

Milford

From Milford comes the story of Ingram Carriage House. This house used to be an inn at one time, and legend has it that suspicious things went on there during its heyday. It is now supposed to be haunted by a couple of "different" ghosts. First there is the ghost that is seen walking down the stairs, and second there is the apparition of a female that is seen upstairs in a nightgown.

The interesting thing about these two ghosts is that people only see half of them. My contact wasn't sure which half of them is seen, but if they conform to most ghosts, then it would have been the bottom half that was missing. Usually, if you see a ghost and their legs or feet are missing, it means the floor has been raised at some time. The typical ghost walks along along at the correct plane for "their" time. If there have been any changes to the structure since then, a ghost will not notice. That is why they are seen to go through walls, for if there was a door there in the past, it will still be there for the ghost.

Lequille

There is another buried treasure tale from around these parts. According to legend, when a group of soldiers left Port Royal they took an amount of gold with them. For safekeeping they buried it somewhere along the Lequille River.

Digby County

Sandy Cove

From Sandy Cove comes the strange story of a man who was abandoned on our shores. In 1864 a foreign ship was spotted off the Digby Neck shore. Local residents had never seen a ship like it before and the next morning they found a man, with his legs amputated below the knees, lying on the beach. The operation that was performed on his legs looked to be professionally done and of recent origin. No information was forthcoming from the victim, however. He refused to speak, except for a word that sounded like Jerome, so that was the name he was given.

Jerome was well-dressed in the best clothes, but any identifying marks had been removed. He was assumed to be of European royalty, and his apparent understanding of English, French, Italian, and other languages seemed to bear this out. Once he was caught off guard when asked where he came from and answered "Trieste." Another time he surprised those taking care of him by giving them the name of his ship, the *Colombo*. Unfortunately, no one seems to have followed up this clue. Even with these hints, no one ever knew for sure who he was or where he came from.

Jerome was taken from Sandy Cove to Metaghan to stay with a local family, then to St. Alphonse de Clare, both of which are across the sound from Sandy Cove. In the forty-eight years of his life spent in these places, Jerome gave no further clues as to his identity. However, there was an incident which added more mystery to the story. He had a visitation with two women who took him into another room away from the family and conversed in an unknown language for a time. This only seemed to add to the rumours that he was of noble birth, and it was thought that these women were sent to make sure he was well in his exile.

After this, no further clues were ever given as to his identity. He died as he arrived, in silence, in 1912.

Tiverton

There is a well-known haunted house in Tiverton where people can be heard walking around upstairs, but on investigation no one can be seen.

Yarmouth County

Carleton

There are at least a couple of resident apparitions in Carleton. From the area known as Clovelly Farm, you can see the ghost of Nathalie, an Acadian girl who attempted to flee the Expulsion and was killed. Also, on June 24, St. Jean Baptiste Day, the figure of a Mi'kmaq man, as well as his footprints, can be seen by the Carleton River.

On Clovelly Farm you can also find five oak trees that have grown together over the years to form a single tree. There is a space in the middle which has filled with water and never goes dry. In fact, it overflows and this is attributed to a Mi'kmaq boy who planted the tree as a symbol of his faith and optimism. The water is believed to have blessed properties.

Darling Lake

Legends circulating around the province about Churchill Mansion speak of mysterious suicides and ghostly occurrences at the picturesque inn, yet the truth is far stranger than this. Incest, slavery, murder and madness all figure into this story.

I'm not sure how the legends began, but this story began in the 1800s when a man named Aaron Churchill was born in Yarmouth. He made his money in the cotton trade and, some insist, the white slave trade as well. He lived in Savannah, Georgia, but he and his entourage would return to Darling Lake almost every year for the summer months and the moverment of his belongings from Yarmouth to Darling Lake was often called a "parade" since it was so long. Rumours suggested that Churchill's daughter was born "not right" and was kept locked in the basement of his Savannah home, and Churchill did indeed leave his daughter behind on these trips. Instead he bought his two nieces and some say they were closer relatives than that. Lottie was his favourite, and he had an "inappropriate" relationship with her. Perhaps it is no wonder that her spirit still has an effect on her summer home.

Local psychics have been consulted about the house, and they seem to always "sense" that old Aaron hasn't left his summer home for good. Visitors who stay in his old bedroom report feeling uneasy and catching a glimpse of an old man in the room. Women seem to sleep easier than men in that room. Most men lie awake all night restless and uneasy.

Stories from the small room next to old man's Churchill's (which will soon be combined with Churchill's to make a large honeymoon suite) include reports of feeling someone or something heavy lying on top of unwary sleepers. In one instance, a key went missing then was mysteriously returned to rest on the visitor's pillow.  One lady visitor rushed downstairs to talk to owner Bob Bezanson and report that as soon as she turned off the light, she felt a heavy pressure on top of her as if a man had climbed into bed with her. On another occasion, a worker at the mansion couldn't find the key to her room anywhere in the tiny room. Tired of looking for it, she locked the door behind her and went downstairs to ask the manager if she could borrow his key to get back in later that day. That was acceptable and the worker spent the day at her tasks, forgetting about the problem key. Upon her return that evening, she borrowed the manager's key, unlocked her door, and walked in to see the missing key lying on her pillow. A check with the manager and staff revealed that no one had entered the room after she left it that morning.

In 1920 Aaron Churchill died at the age of seventy of natural courses. His summer house was bequeathed to his niece Lottie. Her husband was murdered shortly after this and Lottie was committed to McLeans Hospital in Boston, until a house was built for her in Cape Cod. She spent the last thirty years of her life in Cape Cod, attended to by thirteen staff, all paid from Churchill's estate. Some part of her must still remember the summer house, for her picture is very particular where it hangs at the house. It usually hangs in the hall, but when it has been moved to the front area, business at the mansion drops off sharply, as if Lottie has the power to change people's minds about where they would like to stay.

Yarmouth

From Yarmouth comes the story of Rub-A-Dub. It concerns an old inn called Vengeance House. It was named after a British warship and became a popular watering hole in its time. But in 1807, Vengeance House became known for something else. A young girl named Mary Smith experienced the phenomenon of a force that would knock on the head of her bed. In time it would knock on the walls, under her feet, and in response to questions. Many researchers investigated this phenomenon, but no one could explain it away. Eventually, Mary Smith died and the inn was torn down.

Murder Island

Of all the names in Nova Scotia this one has to be one of the strangest and most unsettling. And it has some unsettling stories to go along with its name.

It was in the 1700s that the stories began. It was said that human skulls could be seen lying on the beach, bleached white by the sun and sea. During the 1800s there were said to be hundreds of bodies lying on the beach.

Various theories were advanced for these sightings. It was said that perhaps some of the skulls or bodies were the result of clashes between settlers and Mi'kmaq, or perhaps sick people from passing ships were let off to die on the lonely shore. Oak Island was also mentioned, the popular theory being that the workers drafted to dig the assorted tunnels on Oak Island would have been killed in order to protect the momentous secret. It was on Murder Island that the executions would have taken place. Whatever the correct theory to explain the grisly findings, Murder Island is not a place to visit on dark and stormy nights.

Shelburne County

Mud Island

On December 18, 1883, a vicious storm hit the area and a brig bound for New York, the *Amaranth*, anchored here. Five sailors and a woman were swept overboard during the storm, and their bodies lost until days later. They were buried and forgotten until years later, when excavations were being carried out and workmen suddenly happened upon a grisly find.

The body of the woman had turned to stone. Her body was as white as marble and very lifelike, and she became known as the Petrified Woman. This curiosity drew quite a few crowds until the residents of the island reburied her in a secret grave so that she, and they, would get some peace.

Cape Sable Island

In 1976 stories emerged about an enormous sea serpent seen off the coast. The creature was described as having two tusks that hung down from its upper jaw. It also had large red saucer-like eyes, and was estimated to be between forty to fifty feet long, grey, and heavily barnacled. Its tail was also described as being fish-like, not whale-like. This particular monster was only seen for a few days, though as reports from other parts of the world prove, these mysterious "somethings" can and do return from time to time.

Shag Harbour

From Shag Harbour comes an interesting story that may be one of ufology's greatest mysteries. Some even believe it is more important than the alleged crash of a UFO reported in Roswell, New Mexico, in 1947.

Shortly after eleven p.m. on October 4, 1967, a large unidentified object with amber-coloured lights was seen descending towards Shag Harbour. Witnesses believed the object was about to plunge into the water, but it was seen to float on the sea less than one thousand feet from the shore, apparently drifting with the tide.

The witnesses notified the local Royal Canadian Mounted Police detachment and they sent two cruisers to the area to investigate. The object was estimated to be sixty feet wide, and about ten feet high with a single pale yellow light noticeable. The RCMP and original witnesses believed the craft to be a downed plane and were now concerned with any possible survivors. But before they could notify Search and Rescue in Halifax, or begin to respond with local boats, the object slipped beneath the waves. However, police and several fishermen did set out for the last known location of the "craft" and were surprised to find a half-mile-long foamy trail floating on the water about a mile offshore.

The search for "survivors" from the downed "plane" came up empty and about an hour later a Canadian Coast Guard cutter came on the scene. About this time, SAR Halifax reported that all commercial, military and private aircraft were accounted for all the way along the eastern seaboard.

The search then officially ended, but many questions remained. The official RCMP documents and reports referred to the object as a UFO, and the Royal Canadian Air Force also called it a crashed UFO. In the following year the Condon Report on UFOs would refer to this crash as Case #34 and classify it as unsolved after looking at all other possible explanations, i.e. meteors, crashed space hardware, etc.

Cape Negro

Stories are told here of a fully rigged sailing ship, ablaze in light, with no one on board, sailing the local waters.

Shelburne

From Shelburne comes the story of a poltergeist that haunted the Gill family throughout the early 1970s. It consisted mostly of strange noises and the sound of things being moved, with no evidence of such. It became more pronounced when the children were left alone, as is the case with most poltergeists.

Also from Shelburne harbour comes part two of the Shag Harbour incident. Apparently the object that crash-landed at Shag Harbour moved underwater up the coast to the outer reaches of Shelburne harbour. Also at that location was a super-secret submarine location and tracking station. Needless to say, this alerted high officials in the Canadian and American governments.

Soon military units from both countries showed up at Shelburne. American and Canadian navy ships were offshore, and dive teams were sent to the bottom to investigate this foreign/alien object. All this activity got the Soviets interested and soon Soviet subs were in the area and had to be shooed away.

Although many of the people involved are reluctant to speak, some details have come to light. Apparently there were two objects in the area, one "helping" the other. The objects were not believed to be Soviet or other Communist Bloc vessels. Rumours circulated that the objects were tracked for seven days as they moved towards the Maine coast and then disappeared. There is the possibility that this was some secret "black" operation of one of the American intelligence organizations, although some of the Canadian divers who will speak off the record believe that the objects were alien spacecraft.

Mystic Farm

Running between the #103 and #3 highways outside of Shelburne is the Jordan Branch Road. From here comes the story of an elderly ghost named Nina who haunts a picturesque place called Mystic Farm. Nina is a former owner of Mystic Farm, and she has decided to stay around and keep looking after the old homestead.

The present owners of Mystic Farm know when Nina is around, for she announces her presence with the traditional cold spot or sometimes with the smell of smoke. On occasion, the owners even catch sight of Nina making her rounds, and they have become quite used to her by now. The second ghost, however, is another matter.

Whereas Nina is content to quietly go about her business, the second ghost makes its presence known by incessantly knocking on the back door. It is believed the outside ghost is that of a young man who died in a car accident nearby, and is seeking assistance from beyond the grave.

Queens County

Fort Point, Liverpool

Dexter's Tavern was built in 1763 just as the large migration of the New England Planters began to wind down. As the name suggests, it was originally used as a tavern and inn, although now it is a private residence. The house was built using trees from the area, but the basement was built with large, heavy stones that some believe came from Louisbourg after it was taken by the English. Perhaps this explains the presence of the ghost. Although it is heard more than seen, when visible the ghost is that of a small man in uniform who walks back and forth in the master bedroom. A chill will sometimes precede his appearance and he has been known to open locked doors and cause knocking sounds from time to time. He is seen as a friendly presence and causes no fear in the residents of the house. (I am especially grateful to

Carol Matthews-Horsley for allowing me access to her original 1973 report on Dexter's Tavern.)

Outside of Liverpool Bay there have been reports of a sea monster, which would make a day of sailing quite exciting, I imagine. Nova Scotia has a long list of reports of both aquatic monsters and ghost ships, with almost every town or port having at least one.

Sandy Cove

The Tan Brook in Sandy Cove is haunted by the apparition of a calf with luminous eyes like ball lightning. There was also a sighting of a mysterious man who appeared and disappeared with a clap of thunder.

Lunenburg County

Lunenburg

Gallows Hill is reputed to be the burial ground for a werewolf that was spotted in December 1755. Animals were found torn apart and mysterious shadows lurked outside in the bushes of many a home. A local man was found covered with blood, snarling like a mad dog, and had to be subdued by a group of men. The man apparently murdered his own child and was secured in the local jail. The next morning he was found dead, having ripped out the veins in his arms. The burial place is not marked, but an old timer might have an idea, passed down through generations, of where to find his grave.

Blockhouse Creek Bridge

Here, it is said a murdered woman, clad in white, eternally runs from her attackers.

Teaser Light

One June night in 1813 an American privateer, *Young Teaser*, was chased by British warships into Mahone Bay. The captain torched the magazine and the ship blew up. Since that time, some have seen a blazing ship sailing the bay at night during June and December. The December apparition could be related to the predecessor of the *Young Teaser*, the *Teaser*, which was burned by British ships six months before the *Young Teaser* met her fate. There are also stories of a ball of fire crossing the bay, so it is possible both ships are making an appearance in the still of the night.

Chester

There are many fine inns along the South Shore, and some of the most intersting are those around Chester. One in particular boasts more than its share of charm, if you find a ghost a charming addition, that is.

Haddon Hall sits atop a hill overlooking the town, but it is not as scary looking as the many haunted houses Hollywood portrays sitting in similar situations. There are not winding roads with dead trees leading up to the inn, but there is a resident ghost to keep you company. Staff at the inn believe the ghost to be a former owner of the inn who stops by on occasion to keep an eye on her former residence. She is also said to watch the cleaning staff to make sure they do a good job. She has even been credited with warning the owner that her pet cockatoo was in danger of freezing to death.

Martin's Point

In Martin's Point there resides in one of the older houses a tired ghost that sits at the edge of the bed. And a former nunnery is haunted by the ghost of a Father Broom who hung himself there.

Oak Island

Perhaps Nova Scotia's most renowned mystery is that of Oak Island. More precisely, it is the treasure rumoured to be buried on Oak Island that has captured the world's imagination. For two hundred years many people have searched and dug, and spent much money on this quest. This is their story.

In 1795 Daniel McInnis visited the island one day as a lark. Oak Island was mostly trees then, although some logging had been performed on the island. After walking through the forest, the teenager came upon a clearing. The clearing wasn't new, however, since saplings were growing in place of the trees that were cut down. In the middle of the clearing was an old oak tree that had a branch which extended over a small depression in the ground. Accounts differ, but some say that there was an old tackle block hanging from the tree which crumbled to the ground when touched.

Daniel realized there was something buried there. Since Nova Scotia's coastline was often the haunt of many a pirate, he made the connection with treasure that has never been broken. The next day he returned with two friends by the name of Vaughan and Smith and they pro-ceeded to dig out the hole. On that day, the Money Pit, as it became known, began to capture their imagination and weave a complicated web.

The boys dug down to a level of ten feet before they reached a floor of decaying logs. Excited at this discovery, they pulled up the logs to discover more dirt below. Again they dug and at the twenty foot level they again reached a platform of logs. Again they pulled these up and again

DATE	GROUP	DISCOVERIES
1803-04	Onslow Company	12' x 12' chamber at 100 feet
1849-51	Truro Company	possible chests, pieces of gold chain, built coffer dam to attempt to block sea tunnel
1861-64	Oak Island Association	proved treasure chamber had dropped into large cavern
1866-67	Oak Island Eldorado Company	tried to use coffer dam to block sea tunnel
1878	Sophie Sellers	
1893-1900	Oak Island Treasure Company	cave-in pit, second water tunnel, reached depth of 170 feet
1909	Old Gold Salvage & Wrecking Company	drilled to 167 feet
1931	Chappell	miner's seal oil lamp, axe head, pick and anchor fluke
1936-38	Hedden	stone triangle, collapsed water-tunnel
1938-44	Edwin H. Hamilton	explored water tunnels
1955	George J. Greene	pumped 100,000 gallons of water into pit which vanished
1959-65	Robert Restall	found drains at the beach Restall, his son and two others died of fumes in the pit
1965-66	Robert Dunfield	practically dug out the island
1966–present	Triton Alliance	a chest and a floating hand were observed via TV around 170 feet

there was dirt underneath. They finally dug down to the thirty foot level and after pulling that platform of logs up they decided they needed more help. However, it wasn't until 1805 that they were able to convince people to give up their time and effort in a treasure hunt. And when they did, all they found were more platforms of logs and a stone tablet that had mysterious markings on it. Some have tried to decipher the markings and one translation read, "Ten feet below, £2 million are buried."

Over the years many investors and groups started out with high hopes and good strategies, only to find their hopes dashed by a dose of reality. The accompanying table (on page 54) lists the various groups, dates and major discoveries over the last two hundred years.

Also over the years many theories and theorists have come and gone, and the only constant has been the unshakable belief in the existence of a treasure. Regardless of what was actually buried on the island, it was of extreme importance to someone for them to go through the elaborate precautions of protecting it like this. It is unlikely that it is pirates' treasure, as pirates rarely held onto their money or booty long enough to bury it, let alone bury it so elaborately. Here are a few of the many theories that have emerged over the years.

Theory One

Certainly the oldest and most persistent theory of who buried what on Oak Island is that of Captain Kidd. Captain William Kidd was an English privateer who plied the waters of the Atlantic and Caribbean in the 1680s and '90s. In the late 1690s events proved difficult and during an anti-piracy campaign, he strayed over the line into the very act he was out to crush. This, as well as some political manoeuverings and backstabbing, resulted in his arrest and sentence of death at the gallows. Just before he met his fate on May 23, 1701, Kidd wrote to the government informing them that he had hidden a great deal of treasure and, if they would let him live a little longer, he would lead them to it. This effort was in vain, and the sentence of death was carried out. However, this last plea from the condemned man has resulted in many a treasure hunt around the world and given Oak Island a ready culprit for the workings on the island.

Alas, however, it is unlikely Captain Kidd put anything on Oak Island. Firstly, the crews that Captain Kidd had were a mutinous, criminal bunch with little discipline, certainly not the discipline necessary to build the Money Pit. Secondly, Captain Kidd's time is almost totally accounted for by historians. There is no gap in the record for the amount of time it took to do what was done on Oak Island, estimated at two years. There is no evidence that Captain Kidd was anywhere near Oak Island at any time.

Theory Two

This is a related one. Some believe that other pirates buried a remarkable treasure on Oak Island. This theory is given some credence by those who know that pirates frequented Nova Scotia, particularly the La Have River farther down the coast. However, the classic scene of pirates burying their treasure is not entirely correct. Pirates spent more treasure than they ever buried, and after the few times they did bury some of their treasure, they often came back for it.

That said, there have been small caches of unidentified treasure found from time to time, but nothing as large as the efforts on Oak Island would seem to indicate. Someone spent a lot of time and effort to hide something very large and/or valuable, not just pickings from some ship. Added to this is the fact that not many pirates had the technical training, time or manpower to do something like Oak Island. Even the idea of a communal bank for pirates doesn't seem logical. Hidden money does no one any good. The whole reason for existence for a pirate was to spend money, not hide it. And it's doubtful that many pirates would trust one another enough to develop a communal bank for their treasure. As a final nail in the pirate communal bank coffin, no whispers or hints of such a thing have ever surfaced, and not all pirates died early deaths.

Theory Three

This theory is really a hard sell. You first have to believe that William Shakespeare didn't really write all those plays attributed to him. The theory is that Sir Francis Bacon did and that he felt he must hide his authorship of the plays for political reasons. Because of his Masonic connections with the major explorers and developers of the New World, he decided to hide the manuscripts on a deserted island far away from palace intrigue.

There is no evidence that Francis Bacon wrote any of Shakespeare's plays and sonnets, though some scholars seem to find it impossible to believe that someone with limited education and no great political connections could write the beautiful works that we believe William Shakespeare produced.

Now, even if I could subscribe to the theory that Francis Bacon really did the writing, I must believe that he buried his manuscripts underground guarded by water tunnels. Paper . . . water, hmm. Doesn't seem logical to me, although some people throw the idea out that the manuscripts were secured in liquid mercury to preserve them. Still, the only evidence for the fact that there is something of a paper product down there is a tiny fragment of parchment brought up with one of the drills. I can think of a simpler reason why there would be parchment down there. Perhaps there would be a manifest listing the total of whatever is down there and perhaps its worth. This would provide a far simpler explanation for finding paper down there.

As for the Masonic connections, practically everyone in power in England at that time and the men they sent out to discover and develop new lands, was a Mason. I don't think you could find an explorer during that time who wasn't a Mason or connected with one.

Theory Four

This theory is almost as complicated as the Bacon one, but at least it has circumstantial evidence backing it up. Essentially, it states that the treasure is from the Knights Templars, a military and religious sect that fought in the Crusades and became so rich that many of the monarchs of Europe went to them in time of need. In the fourteenth century, the King of France convinced the Pope to outlaw the Templars. Thus, in a sneak attack, the king's men stormed their castles and arrested, tortured and killed many of them. At the Templars' stronghold, they were able to hold out long enough to spirit some of their massive treasure away, and it has never been found.

Many Templars headed for Scotland and were welcomed there. In 1395, Prince Henry Sinclair, the Earl of Orkney, likely made a transatlantic journey to Nova Scotia, and some scholars have tried for a connection between the Earl and the Templar treasure. However, nothing is certain, although much of it is plausible and could have happened that way.

In the 1980s, a new theory emerged that said that the Holy Grail was actually the sacred bloodline of Jesus of Nazareth, not a cup or chalice. A variation on the theme of the Templars has them hiding either the Holy

Grail, the chalice of the Last Supper, or the Holy Grail, the bloodline (descendents) of Jesus Christ. There is also a theory that the container holding the Shroud of Turin could also be the fabled Holy Grail. Again, there is much circumstantial evidence to link the Templars to the descendents of Jesus Christ and secret societies, and Samuel de Champlain. Coincidentally, Champlain was meticulous in his charting the region of the Maritimes, yet he became vague in the area around Oak Island. Interesting . . .

Theory Five

This theory holds that a pay ship of the British, French or Spanish navy was caught in a storm and washed ashore near Oak Island. The commanders decided to bury the treasure until they could return with a stronger force. Although pay ships of the various navies did founder along the Atlantic coast of North America, and some French ships did make for Bedford Basin, there is no evidence to directly link any missing money and the diggings on Oak Island.

Theory Six

A variation on theory five is that the French felt their holdings in Acadia were in jeopardy and hid some of their money until things cleared up. Of course when they did, the French were out.

Another variation is that the English did much the same, or hid some of the money they would need to fight the American colonists. If this theory were true, why didn't they ever come back for it? Nova Scotia was always under their control and they could have returned to retrieve the treasure at any time.

Theory Seven

This theory again is very similar to the "hide the stuff until it's safe" theories, except that those burying the treasure wanted it safe from the tax man.

This argument holds that after the Sack of Havana in 1752, the leaders of the successful British invasion-cum-looting of Havana decided to skim off some of the take before sending it back to the king. A variation along these lines is that the king didn't trust his ministers and wanted some money hidden away for a royal emergency. Eventually, however, the money was forgotten. But what of the men who organized and buried the treasure?

Who? What?

I have not included every theory as to who buried what on Oak Island. I purposely left out the fantastic, impossible or ridiculous, and concentrated on the theories that at least had a chance of being right, even if the Bacon one is a real stretch.

The person who dreamed up this adventure, planned and engineered it, and executed the world's greatest secular mystery was most likely military or pseudo-military. By this, I would probably reject the Templars as well as Bacon. This was a military job by either the French or more likely, the British. It took two years and massive manpower to construct a trap for the curious. Obviously, it was designed so the treasure could not be retrieved the same way it was hidden. There is some trick to it and it is possible, even likely, that the treasure ended up a short distance away just under the ground ready for easy access.

The Money Pit is meant as a trap to take the curious off the scent. Even the likely treasure chests found through the drilling were probably a sacrificial lamb in case anyone succeeded in getting down that far. Can you imagine going through all this trouble for two treasure chests? No, whatever was or is on Oak Island must have been massive, either in wealth or importance.

The only way to find out who put the treasure there on the island is to search history for the likely suspects: the men who had the capability and disappeared for about two years. Find them and the reason for their efforts, and you have the treasure, at least in your mind. It is possible that the treasure could only be found by unravelling the clues scattered throughout the island, and perhaps at some time in the past, someone did.

Does it not strike anyone as odd that something of this magnitude could stay a secret for so long? Someone must have told someone. Husbands tell wives or families. Families leave letters or papers behind after deaths. There has never been a mention or whisper of the treasure. We have no idea what it is. Therefore, either the men who buried it did not know what it was they were burying, or else they came back and got it.

Also seen on Oak Island are the ghostly apparitions of sixteenth- and seventeenth-century soldiers. They walk the roads, woods and beaches, still guarding or searching for something.

Pirate apparitions are also seen or heard from time to time on the lonely island. Are they the ones who buried something here, still looking for their treasure?

Marriott's Cove
Here there is a house that has ghostly footsteps that climb the stairs every night, accompanied by a cold spot.

Halifax Regional Municipality

St. Margaret's Bay

In 1845 sightings of a very large "sea serpent" were reported to the local press. The creature was estimated to be a 100-foot long beast that was even sighted by the local reverend.

Hackett's Cove

At Devany's Brook, a headless woman comes out of the water periodically.

Also, in the eastern part of St. Margaret's Bay, the ghostly vision of a Spanish ship appears once a year, sometimes on fire.

Shut-In Island

Shut-In Island was originally known as Chetigne Island, and before that, Pirate's Island. It is the latter name that concerns us here. As we have seen, the South Shore of Nova Scotia was a haven for pirates. Although they usually confined themselves to the area around the LaHave River, stories have come down to us about other areas they may have visited. One is present-day Shut-In Island. Over the years many vessels were wrecked on the island or the reef that joins it to the mainland. Legend has it that some of these ships were pirate ships and their crews were forced to bury their ill-gotten loot on the island until they could arrange to come back and get it.

Another story coming out of Shut-In Island is that there is a mysterious light seen at certain times from the mainland. The reporting of strange lights on the island would seem to be only natural considering its reputation. There has long been a belief that pirates would murder someone and bury them with the treasure so that the ghost of the murdered man would scare anyone away from the treasure. So it is not surprising that some would see a light coming from the island.

Terence Bay

A more recent story from this area concerns an apparition that is seen walking down the center line of the Terence Bay Road. It is an old man who appears suddenly at night, giving a driver just enough time to swerve around him. At times, however, this has been impossible, yet when the distraught motorist walks back to search for a body none can be found.

Indian Harbour

Along this desolate and rocky shore there is said to walk the lonely spirit of a Scottish lady in a blue dress. She came to Nova Scotia to marry and have children by a fisherman who died while at sea, leaving her and her children alone since his family (for reasons unknown) would have nothing to do with them. This apparently haunted her in life, and she has carried these regrets with her from beyond the grave, as she continues to walk, sad and lonely along the coastline.

Ketch Harbour

In Ketch Harbour there is an old glebe house that is now rented out to the public. Local rumour has it that none of the priests will stay at the house, so the Catholic Church of St. Peter's had to begin renting it to the public. The house sat vacant for thirteen years before a couple rented it in 1999. It was shortly after this that strange things began to happen.

Neighbours have reported hearing loud arguments coming from the house during the day when no one in the family has been home. The light in the front porch has been known to flash on and off intermittently whenever there are visitors. The circuit breaker for the furnace trips each evening at ten p.m. sharp.

A "sensitive" was brought to the house early in 2000 and she believes the house is haunted by the ghosts of two priests who once lived there many years ago. Apparently, there is the spirit of an older alcoholic priest, as well as a younger one with a much darker secret. The younger one is the most active, as he seeks forgiveness for his sins. The "sensitive" spoke to him and informed him that she couldn't give him the forgiveness he seeks, but he knows he should turn elsewhere for comfort. The spirit of the older priest is more reclusive and less open to communication from this side. As of this writing in the summer of 2000, the situation has been quiet for a couple of months.

Sambro

It is here at Sambro Light that a Scottish soldier once hanged himself, and his ghost can still be seen, as well as heard, throwing casks around.

Chebucto Head Lighthouse

This lighthouse is now unmanned, like many of Nova Scotia's venerable lighthouses. So it is difficult to determine whether the ghostly lady seen by former tenants still walks the cliffs by the lighthouse. Although not much is known about the ghost, it is surmised that she was a shipwreck victim, due to the worn rope tied around her waist. She has been reported many times walking along the cliffs, and often her presence was detected inside the lighthouse, although she was never seen.

Halifax

Bridge curse

A Mi'kmaq medicine man put a curse on three bridges to be built joining the twin cities of Halifax and Dartmouth. The first was to fall in a storm, the second calmly, and the third in death. The first, a foot bridge, fell in a vicious storm. The second, a railway bridge, dropped into the harbour on a sunny day. The third was to drop in the dead of night. When it came time to open the third bridge, the Angus L. MacDonald Bridge, authorities asked the Mi'Kmaq chief of the time to remove the curse. It apparently has worked. The bridge has stood solidly since it was built in the 1950s.

Bill Lynch Fair curse

All Nova Scotians know the annual Bill Lynch Fair, which comes to Halifax each May. According to legend, an employee of the fair slept with a Mi'kmaq woman, either a chief's wife or daughter. Needless to say, the chief wasn't too pleased and cursed the couple as they made their escape in a boat. He warned that foul weather would follow them wherever they went, and so it is that every May in Halifax when the fair comes to town, rain is sure to follow.

Halifax Harbour approaches

There are two different kinds of sightings in the waters just outside the city. There are reports that on foggy nights a fully rigged sailing vessel is seen sailing into the harbour. There have also been reports of a sea serpent seen just outside the harbour during the last century.

The Robie Street Palace

This white house, second from the intersection of Jubilee Road and Robie Street, heading north along Robie, used to be a manor house on a piece of land encompassing the whole block. It was the residence of the first mayor of Halifax, William Caldwell, and was built in classic Doric style. For years it has had the reputation of being haunted, especially one side of the house, which has a blackened window.

One legend has it that someone hanged himself in the room just behind the blackened window, and ever since that time, the window will turn to black no matter how many times it is changed. Another story says that witches were dancing opposite the window, a resident of the house was caught watching them and they cursed him. Needless to say, many a wide-eyed child has run past this house on a cold, dark night.

The real reason the window is black is because of the Doric style of the house. Immediately behind the window is a dividing wall, causing the window to appear black. The house is haunted though, but not by the spirit of anyone who hanged himself. People have seen an apparition in white. Doors do open and close by themselves and a former occupant found himself nervous many times when he was working late at night.

Queen Elizabeth II Health Sciences Centre

When the New Halifax Infirmary, a part of the QE II Medical Centre, was being built in 1994-95 excavators dug up old graves as they put in the foundations. Strange noises have been reported and rumour has it that it is an old Indian burial ground or military cemetery from the days when the area, called Camp Hill, was a barracks. There are also rumours that strange shapes have been seen in the basement as well as vague stories about the fourth floor. People feel strange and get weird vibrations on that floor.

All Saints Cathedral

This beautiful cathedral has seen more than its share of visitors over the years, including one from beyond the grave.

In 1933, the dean of All Saints Cathedral was hit by a car as he made his way to comfort a parishioner who was at death's door. Instead of comforting the dying parishioner, Dean Llwyd joined him in death two weeks later. Since this time parishioners have spoken of seeing Dean Llwyd, apparently going about his routines as if still blessed with life. He has been seen looking out at his congregation, walking along the altar, and striding up the aisle, still concerned with his earthly duties.

Tower Road School

On December 6, 1917, the largest man-made explosion (prior to the first nuclear explosion) occurred in the "Narrows" section of Halifax Harbour. It blew away most of the North End of Halifax, killed 3,000 people and left many more homeless. Many of the injured were taken to city schools and Tower Road School was utilized as a makeshift morgue. The apparition of a male teenager has been seen climbing the stairs to the attic, as well as walking through the basement. Footsteps are also heard in the deserted school and legend has it the ghost is that of a teenager killed in the Halifax Explosion and brought there for processing. Maybe he was unidentified and is still waiting for his family to come and claim him.

Old Mission to Seamen House

At the south end of Barrington Street is a house that at one time was a mission to seamen and is now a business residence. In an office that was once the chapel, burning incense can still be smelled and the image of a big man can be seen.

Brewery Market

Today the Brewery Market is filled with small shops, atriums, restaurants and offices, but it began as the brewing house for Alexander Keith, a famous brew-master of Nova Scotia. Even though he has been dead for many, many years, his ghost has been seen walking through the complex by some of the caretakers.

St. Paul's Anglican Church

During the Halifax Explosion of 1917 many buildings were damaged in the downtown. One of them was St Paul's, one of the oldest churches in North America. It still bears scars from the explosion, including a piece of metal from the *Mont Blanc*, the French munitions ship which collided with the *Imo*, causing the explosion.

There is another scar that the church is known for, however. One of the glass windows on Argyle Street was broken, and the silhouette of a man wearing a high hat can be seen. Local legend has it that the head of the parish minister went through the window during the explosion, but officials at the church would only say that the image bears an uncanny likeness to the minister at that time.

Ghostly party at the Admiral's Residence

This story came to me from the daughter of an admiral who stayed in the residence a few years ago. The house is tucked away on the piece of land bordered by Queen, Sackville and Brunswick Streets; the building itself is set back from Sackville Street.

A few years ago this woman was sleeping one night while her parents were out to a military function. Waking up just after midnight, she heard the sounds of a party

downstairs and assumed her parents had brought some friends and colleagues home. She went back to sleep, and the next morning casually mentioned it to her parents, who denied bringing anyone back with them. Not being able to convince them it hadn't been a dream, she put it in the back of her mind and almost forgot about it — until the uninvited guests made themselves known again.

Occasionally, the ghostly party would start in the middle of the night, usually just after midnight. On a few occasions, the revellers were heard by the admiral and his wife, as well as by the daughter. No one was able to surprise the "guests" in the act, or determine the period of the party, so the events remain an intriguing mystery.

Old NSCAD School

Before the Nova Scotia College of Art and Design moved to its present location downtown, it resided on Coburg Road. In the old photocopier room there was seen the ghost of a student who took sick and died on the way to the hospital. Dalhousie University owns the building now and it houses the Faculty of Management.

Shirreff Hall

Shirreff Hall is the women's residence at Dalhousie University, and new students soon become aware of the distinguished university's resident ghost. Penelope is her name, and although careful research has failed to turn up a girl by that name who ever worked there, ask anyone around the residence and they will tell you she is there now.

A cold blast of air greets students on the fourth floor of Shirreff Hall, and the shade of Penelope is seen walking down the hallway or standing at the foot of students' beds. Penelope allegedly hanged herself in the attic and it is said the rope is hanging there still. Whatever despair she felt in life drives Penelope to revisit the familiar surroundings in death.

Prince's Lodge

In the early years of Halifax there came to these shores Prince Edward, Duke of Kent, later to become father of Queen Victoria. He made his home on the edge of Bedford Basin with a grand mansion, heart-shaped pond, long trails through the woods, and a beautiful rotunda, called the Round House. The Prince, however, was not without company. He had taken a French mistress, and it was for her that the heart-shaped pond and rotunda were built. In later years Edward was forced to give up his mistress when he became king, but for a few years there were many romantic nights by the shore in Halifax. But there is a darker side of the story.

The Prince and his mistress entertained often, and during one of these soirées a Colonel Olgolvie and a Captain Howard got into a heated argument. This led to a duel early one morning after the party, even though the Prince had forbidden all such duels. Both men died of their wounds, and the Prince was not amused. He ordered that the body of Colonel Olgolvie be buried where it fell, just below the beautiful Round House. They say that the ghost of the dead colonel still wanders the grounds of the Round House, and will continue to do so until he has had a proper burial.

Historic Properties

Historic Properties is a collection of old buildings on the Halifax waterfront that have been restored to their original condition. They are a great tourist attraction with many shops, restaurants, bars and offices. They also have a few ghosts. In one building in particular (where the Lower Deck Lounge is located), there is a ghostly shadow of a man that is seen in the offices when they are almost deserted and quiet. There have also been whisperings of other entities having been seen over the years, but they are proving harder to track down. But during a typical foggy Halifax night when the mist is heavy upon the ground and sound reverberates between the ancient buildings, the ghosts may be easy to find.

Halifax Library

The Halifax Library on Spring Garden Road is an old and atmospheric place. There is a statue of Sir Winston Churchill on the lawn out front, and the whole area is a beautiful place for Haligonians and street musicians to hang out on warm and bright days. But inside it is a different story. Reports come to us that the library has its resident ghost. Although many libraries report a ghost of a former librarian, this ghost is not so identified. But it is a ghost. People report seeing shapes and shadows of people who couldn't possibly be there or disappear so quickly. The building has a great deal of twists and turns with shadowy corners for ghosts or anyone to hide in.

Five Fishermen Restaurant

The Five Fishermen Restaurant is one of the finer eating estalishments in the province, and this author has spent many a birthday meal enjoying the excellent food and hospitality, quite unaware that he could have been watched over by the resident ghost.

The spirit that is said to reside in the restaurant is a ghost with an attitude. Most ghosts are content to quietly maintain their presence but this one lets the staff know when it is around. It has been heard to call out a staff member's name, trip others, and it has even trapped one employee in a room.

1361 Barrington Street

Presently this building is occupied by the Nova Scotia Association of Architects, NSAA. But previously it housed the medical offices of a dermatologist, and before that the house served as a private residence. When the building was a doctor's office, many of the staff refused to go up-stairs because of the recurring ghostly cries of a baby that could be heard. Also, many of the pictures that were hung refused to stay on the walls and would be found laying on the floor. This was more than enough for the staff to avoid the upstairs like the plague.

Waverley Inn

The Waverley Inn on Barrington Street is diagonally across the street from the NSAA building and is one of the more charming inns in Halifax. A famous guest appears from time to time, over a hundred years after he visited the city in the flesh.

Oscar Wilde was a household name when he visited Halifax in the late 1800s. The famous British dramatist and poet was beginning a North American tour, and the Waverley Inn was where he stayed while in Halifax. Wilde was a flamboyant character, both in dress and mannerisms, and must have made quite the impression on Haligonians. Obviously they made a lasting impression on him, for he promised to return to Halifax one day, and although he didn't keep that promise while alive, he has kept it after death. Staff and visitors have reported seeing an apparition that is garishly dressed, often reading a book, and in the room they say Wilde occupied while here over a hundred years ago.

The Halifax Club

The Halifax Club is one of Halifax's oldest and most prestigious clubs. No one knows for sure how many ghosts are at the Halifax Club, or who they are. There are stories of a member who killed himself and another who died while cheating on his wife, and some suspect these two may be responsible for some of the supernatural activity. But there is also a female presence there, so perhaps it is the repentant mistress of the cheating member. After he expired, it is said, she put him in a cab and sent him to the club. Perhaps they are together again in death.

Also believed to haunt the premises are a mother and son, although no one has any clue as to why they call the Halifax Club home. Some of the phenomena reported includes the smell of tobacco smoke and shadows moving up the stairs. After a major fire in 1995, workmen would hear the sounds of people walking up the stairs, or running on the second floor, even though there was no one else in the building. Most of the phenomena occurs between midnight and seven in the morning, so apparently the ghosts like to have the place to themselves.

Maritime Museum of the Atlantic

The museum has only been in its present location since 1982, but already it has its share of lingering spirits and ghostly phenomena. For years, staff have grown accustomed to turning off the lights, only to find them switched back on shortly afterwards. There have also been reports of ghostly footsteps and scuffing noises, particularly on the second and third floors, and rumours that a staff member or two may have quit prematurely due to the ghosts.

There are believed to be two spirits haunting the museum. One is said to be that of James Farquhar, a mariner whose statue once graced a window overlooking the foyer. Staff complained that the eyes of the statue followed them as they walked by, so it was moved to a less visible location.

The other spirit is said to be that of soldier Alex Alexander, who lived during the American Revolution and was responsible for guarding the Sambro Lighthouse. He did not die in battle, but in shame. Given the responsibility to go to Halifax and procure supplies, he wasted the money on drink instead. Upon returning to the lighthouse, he hanged himself. His ghost was said to haunt the lighthouse for years, and now it is said his spirit has followed the Sambro light to its quarters at the museum. Perhaps it is his footsteps that are heard here late at night.

Richmond Street School

This school now houses the Family Court and is located on Devonshire Avenue. It is haunted by a ghost called Peggy. The school was severely damaged during the Halifax Explosion of 1917, so perhaps Peggy comes to us from those times.

Fairview Cemetery

This cemetery has some of the remains from the *RMS Titanic*, which struck an iceberg on the night of April 14, 1912, and went down with more than 1,500 souls aboard. Although there have never been any legends concerning the *Titanic* graves, another tomb in the cemetery is called the "Devil's Grave." It is an old grave built into the edge of a hill which has a tree growing on top of it. As the name would suggest, it has the reputation of being the final resting place of Satan.

Bedford/Sackville/Beaverbank/Waverley

These areas have long been seen as the suburbs of Halifax/Dartmouth and are primarily residential. The following stories from these areas are to be found in the little book, *Cries at Kinsac Corner and Other Legends*, written by the students of one of the grade nine classes at Sackville Heights Junior High in the 1970s.

Bedford Basin

As you travel along the scenic Bedford Highway between Halifax and Bedford, stop and roll your window down. You may hear the sounds of muffled oars and straining men as they spend eternity trying to get ashore.

Parker's Brook/Eagle Rock/Spruce Island

In the mid-1800s American visitors would often stay at Bedford for the avowed purpose of looking for buried treasure. These three areas were the most commonly investigated sites, but no one ever found any treasure.

Miller's Lake

This story come to us from Miller's Lake. A railwayman lost his right arm to a train one day and then turned into a bitter recluse. Few people ever saw him, but over the years various people would disappear and never be found. When some hikers happened upon the recluse's cabin one day they were horrified to find the right arms of several people, but no recluse. When the authorities arrived, they found the evidence as well as signs that the recluse had fled with a few belongings and a blue lantern. From that time onward stories would be told of a mysterious blue light seen along the lake and up the mountain alongside of it.

Springfield Lake

During the night observers can see a light gliding across the lake. If you are unfortunate enough to get close to the light, you will see that it is the ghost of a woman who was murdered many years ago by her husband, who threw her from their boat in the middle of the lake. Her ghost still keeps watch, hoping one day to find her husband and exact revenge for her murder.

There is another ghostly woman who reportedly haunts this lake. She is looking for her fiancé, not in anger but in grief. Apparently he drowned in the lake before their wedding day and she died of grief over her loss. She is now said to glide across the lake in her wedding gown, drenched in blood and carrying a lantern as she searches endlessly for him.

Beaverbank

Reportedly, from the Rawdon Road northeasterly through the woods to Enfield, runs a series of tracks that local legend has dubbed "the Devil's Footprints." They are said to have been left by the Devil as he walked through the woods carrying a bag of gold. The tracks run up to one side of Grand Lake, then resume on the other side as if the maker just walked on or under the lake. Many people have searched for the "gold" that the Devil brought with him, but so far they haven't been successful.

Fultz House Museum

This 138-year-old house at the corner of Sackville Drive and Cobequid Road was, for most of its history, the unremarkable residence of Bennett Fultz and his wife Mary. Now it is a musuem maintained by the Fultz Corner Restoration Society and the scene of an ongoing haunting.

For years the staff at the Petro Canada gas station across the street have reported that lights have come on at the museum late at night after all they staff have gone for the day. This most often occurs after midnight, and has been reported for more than fifteen years. The electrical system has been checked out but no obvious problem exists to cause the lights to come on by themselves and only after midnight.

Some visitors have reported sensing an other-worldy presence in the house, and footsteps have been heard on the hardwood floors after visiting hours. Once one of the members of the Fultz Corner Restoration Society was working alone in his office when he heard the back door open, then close, followed by the sounds of footsteps walking down the hall leading to the stairs to the second floor. Calling out, the member received no reply and went in search of the culprit. He quickly found he was alone in the house and his experience is not uncommon. It is said that many people have died in the house since Mary Fultz acted as a nurse for residents in the surrounding area. Perhaps those unfortunate souls still roam the place where they died. Or perhaps it is Mary, endlessly walking the hall still in search of someone to help.

Cobequid Road railway crossing ghost

This story originally took place early in the 1900s, but recently evidence has come to light that perhaps the long-quiet ghost has reappeared, possibly because of the soon-to-be hundredth anniversary.

The tale goes that children were playing near the railway crossing at Cobequid Road when they noticed a strange lady walking along the tracks. Their attention was soon caught by the approach of a train. By the time they looked back towards the woman, she had disappeared —

although she had been out of sight for only a few seconds. Returning home later in the day, they told their parents about what they had seen.

By the children's description of the woman, the parents were able to determine she was someone who had died a few years previously. Her husband worked for the railway company at the time. The next day, he was killed by a train at the same spot where the children had seen his ghostly wife twenty-four hours before. Recently, I have heard stories that the ghost is restless again and can be seen walking along the tracks near the crossing.

Lewis Lake

There is a legend that a cabin once stood near Lewis Lake in Upper Sackville, and that anyone who occupied the cabin was treated to a visit by the ghost of an old lady called The Lady of the Lake. Apparently she would materialize in front of the startled owners and in one case she was said to have written a message on the wall, instructing the occupants to leave.

Hawkin Hill Lake

This lake is reportedly haunted by two ghosts, both pedlars or drifters who came to an untimely end earlier this century. Apparently jealousy sprang up between these men and one of them murdered the other. However, legend has it that the murdered man's ghost drowned the murderer when he tried to dispose of the body of his friend in the lake. Now both ghosts haunt the place where they died.

Maroon Hill

Today on Maroon Hill stands Beacon House, a second hand clothing store. Originally Beacon House was the Sackville Central School and began as a school for black children. Local legend has it that the school was built on land owned by a reclusive lady, who left instructions in her will that a school be built for black children on her land. This was done, but with the passage of time it became necessary for white children to attend the school. This apparently did not sit well with the spirit of the lady benefactor. She reportedly manifested writing on the wall and a pair of ghostly hands that were seen floating in space. She must have gotten used to the idea of white children attending the school though, since there have been no recent manifestations of her displeasure.

Windsor Highway/Jubilee Lane

The intersection of the Number 1 Highway, known as the Windsor Highway, and Jubilee Lane is reported to be the resting place of a woman whose husband loved her so much he buried her on their property which bordered the road. There have been reports of groaning and even sightings of a mysterious light seen nearby.

Waverley Road

Throughout the United States and Canada there is an urban legend about a phantom hitchhiker who is picked up by an unknowing good samaritan and gives instructions as to where he or she wishes to be dropped off. Some versions say the hitchhiker gets out at a cemetery, others say at a house, and still others say that the hitchhiker disappears from the backseat of the car. When the driver goes to the door of the house mentioned by the ghostly guest, he or she is informed that the hitchiker died many years ago and is still trying to get home. Although this legend is mostly just that, there appears to be a true story that started the legend in the 1930s in Arkansas.

Nova Scotia has its version of this legend which takes place on the Waverley Road. It differs from the urban legends only in that it is the good samaritan who is the ghost.

The story goes that the ghost of a truck driver named Joe Santos still drives his truck along the Waverley Road. His truck was named the Phantom 309, and Joe was killed in it in an accident many years ago. In the mid-1960s reports surfaced that people were picked up by this man who identified himself as Joe Santos. Later these hitchhikers were to learn that the man they accepted a drive from had been dead some years.

Blue Pond

It might be a little difficult to get to this location since this pond is reported to be deep in the woods of Beaverbank. However, it has been twenty years since the legend was written down, so the pond may be more accessible now that the area is more developed.

Legend has it there is a pond in Beaverbank with water so blue that it gave the pond its name. Apparently a strange egg was found one day and it continued to grow larger and larger until it was dumped into the pond. From that egg emerged a "large, scaly, green serpent or dragon." This dragon is still said to haunt the pond and carry off the unwary visitor.

Devil's Island, Halifax Harbour

Devil's Island must have the most stories in the whole area. There definitely are some strange happenings on that now abandoned island. Strange fires, ghostly footsteps and visitations from the devil all abound here.

Devil's Island is reputed to conceal buried treasure, but it rests in a bottomless pit so no one has been able to get to it yet.

There used to be a lake in the middle of the island, but it was drained in order to search for treasure supposedly sunk there.

A resident of Devil's Island was found decapitated one morning after apparently meeting the Devil himself.

McNab's Island, Halifax Harbour

McNab's Island is one of the last areas of almost unspoiled beauty in Halifax. It has been used as a gallows to hang pirates and has had fortifications on it to defend the city, but it is mostly overgrown now. The island has hiking trails and is accessible only by boat. But it is still occupied by ghosts.

The name McNab's comes from Peter McNab, who once owned the island. He is still there to this day. Upon his death he was buried on the island he loved so much, but legend has it they buried his body on one end of the island, with his head buried on the opposite end. To this day his spirit is seen walking the length of the island looking to reclaim his head.

There was once an orphanage on this island which one night burned down. The fire was caused by a candle that got too close to a curtain. Many children were injured or killed and their anguished and frightened cries are said to echo throughout the island. Reports also come down to us of a floating candle seen near the ruins of the orphanage.

There are also reports of a ghostly horse and carriage that is heard making its way across the island on one of the lonely roads.

And finally, this story was given to me by Jamie Cox, whose friend regularly boats over to the island. One time the friend's brother was waiting in the boat as it was tied up at the dock. He was startled by sounds of something scraping the length of the underside of the boat. Needless to say he quickly vacated the boat and much later when they brought the boat up onto a dock in Halifax, they saw the keel had been scraped as if by claws . . .

South East Passage

There was a house here that became quite famous during World War II, when a poltergeist and ghost made their appearance. Strange knocks, clothes being torn off their owners and items being thrown around unnerved the residents. The house was only three years old, but the owners tore it down and built a new one nearby.

Dartmouth Shore

There are legends of buried treasure somewhere along the Dartmouth shore — treasure buried by Spanish pirates, although no exact location is known.

95 King Street, Dartmouth

Although no confirmed ghosts reside here, there are a couple of mysteries connected with it. The house was owned in the mid-1800s by Dr. John MacDonald, Governor of Dalhousie College and a Justice of the Peace. He was also a respected businessman, so it was a surprise in 1846 when he vanished off the face of the earth. There have never been any concrete leads as to where he went, although foul play was most likely the reason. In 1879, there was a skull found buried under the basement of the house. Popular legend had it that the skull belonged to one of the Saladin Pirates who were hanged in 1844. Perhaps if modern DNA testing had been available it would have been discovered that the skull was that of Dr. MacDoanld, the former owner of the house.

Seaforth

If you ask nicely one of the locals here may tell you in which house the Gray Lady floats down the staircase to greet her guests.

Petpeswick Harbour

From here comes a story of a Norwegian barque that is sighted before a storm. Sometimes it appears as the ship, at other times it is just a ball of light.

Oyster Pond

Another mysterious ghost ship is seen here. A fully rigged ship sometimes sails up the harbour, and voices speaking in an unknown language are sometimes heard across the water.

There are also sightings of a headless woman, dressed in white, who supposedly knows the whereabouts of buried treasure.

Goose Island

From here comes the sound of a ghostly rowboat that is never seen.

Pleasant Harbour

Yet another phantom ship legend. Apparently there is a ghostly ship that sails into Pleasant Harbour on a clear night. Unlike many ghost ships, this one is fully manned and an observer can hear the crew talking in some strange language as the ship sails right up to the shore and disappears into the woods.

Mushaboom

Another ghostly sailing ship sails across the waters and even through ice in winter.

Sheet Harbour

Before you reach the town of Sheet Harbour, the road curves around the actual harbour. As you drive, remember the legend that somewhere along the road across from the town, a section is known as the Ghost Road. Back in 1899 locals would hear the wails of the dead, and coffins and human shapes were seen along the road.

Sable Island

It is unlikely you will actually be able to go out to Sable Island in person, unless you happen to be in the gas and oil industry. The island is about a hundred miles off the coast of Nova Scotia and quite isolated, except for the odd gas exploration vessel passing by. A few hundred years ago the story was very different. Sable Island was given the name "Graveyard of the Atlantic" because of all the ships that were wrecked upon her shores. The treacherous currents, coupled with dense fogs and the unpredictable weather of the North Atlantic, served to dash many a captain's hopes and many lives. Needless to say, with all this death and destruction there are resident ghosts on the island.

One is the vision of a woman who is missing one finger. Her name was Mrs. Copeland and she was a passenger on the ship *Frances* which went down in 1799. There is some dispute as to whether the lady was murdered or not, but legend has it that one of her fingers was cut off to get at a gold ring. Tales have come down about her pitiful ghost roaming the island searching for her missing finger.

Guysborough County

Little Harbour

The British ship *Billow* sank in a storm in 1830. To this day the residents say that when the wind blows right, you can hear the ship's band playing "The Gay Cockade."

Marshes

Willie, the drunk, still walks these marshes with his ghostly lantern, trying to lure unsuspecting people to their doom.

Strait of Canso

Somewhere along the Strait is Nova Scotia's only merman. I have heard these stories from a few different places, so it must be more than a fish story. There is no word on any female company for him yet.

Pirate Harbour

Captain Kidd reportedly spent one winter around here to escape capture by warships. Legend has it he buried treasure here and a black man was murdered in order to guard the treasure. The brook where the man's spirit still roams is called Black Peter's Brook.

Richmond County

Port Hawkesbury

Two haunted houses can be found in Port Hawkesbury. On Philpott Street there is a house which is haunted by hallway lights turning on and off. Musty smells alternate with the smell of sulphur or sweet perfume. A second house is known by the locals for its cold spots and the spectres of a mother and her child.

Port Malcolm Bay

Many years ago, back in the age of sail, a ship sank in a storm and to this day, when the wind blows from the southeast, you can hear the screams of victims.

Glasgow Point

There is an apparition of a headless skater, wearing a long flowing gown, that haunts the area. The ghost is one of two girls who were drowned here one winter day. No one has reported seeing the ghost of the other drowned skater, but there are also reported sightings of strange lights seen on cold dark nights.

Groz Nez Island

Stories are still told of a light that can be seen in any weather, far off in the distance on Groz Nez Island. The tales originated before the time of electricity and though not as frequent now, some say it still shines in the lonely distance from time to time.

Port Michaud

In 1745 the French frigate *St Michel*, loaded with gold and silver, was on its way to the great French fortress of Louisbourg. She was almost caught up in the battle raging between the British and French over Louisbourg, but luck was with her and she escaped, only to run aground off of Port Michaud. There was never any official attempt at salvaging the wreck, so a vast fortune still lays somewhere offshore. However, before you get excited and go diving for the treasure, be forewarned that there were sightings of a soldier standing guard near the wreck, and he was believed by some to be an apparition of one of those who died and is still doing his duty.

The Black Ground

The Black Ground is an uninhabited, wide-open space, with the ruins of old foundations and ancient paths, bordered by a lake and tall spruces. No one seems able to live there for very long, and from dense overgrowth above comes piercing cries of unseen birds of prey. Strange grunts from unknown animals and other hard-to-pin-down sounds emanate from it. Human shapes appear at will. Some of them are distant and indistinct, but others are sharp and clear. Both, however, exist in another time, for they ignore people of our time and can't be approached. There are rumours of hidden treasure and maybe that is what those mysterious apparitions are searching for.

French Cove

It is here that a British ship is said to have buried gold that was to be used for paying their soldiers. Apparently there were too many French troops so the Brits thought that burying the gold would be the wisest course of action. They were right, since just after they buried the gold, they were attacked by pirates who destroyed the ship. It is said the pirates got some of the gold, but not all of it. The rest lies buried somewhere in the vicinity.

Cape Breton County

Blackett's Lake

Strange stories come from around here and some people have noted that the area just "feels" wrong to them.

There is a story told about a girl who lived in Ontario and took a plane to Sydney, then a taxi to Blackett's Lake. When she arrived at the lake she proceeded to drown herself, leaving no note or reason why. The strangest aspect to the story is that she did not know anyone in Cape Breton, nor had she been here before.

Other reports come to us that Coxheath Mountain, whose slopes lead to the lake, has odd geological properties, for many compasses will not function properly, and strange lights and screams have also been seen and heard around here. Strange lights are also seen over the lake and surrounding areas. Terrible screams and the sense of being followed are common to those who dare walk aound here at night.

Louisbourg

In its heyday Louisbourg was France's greatest fortress in the New World. It was certainly the greatest threat to the British Empire and so Britain launched two major battles to conquer the fortress. Both times the British won, but after the first battle the British had to cede the fort back to the French. During these seesaw times many ships were entering and leaving Louisbourg, and many were wrecked either in the harbour or in its approaches. Over the years some of these wrecks have been found, and some money and treasure recovered, but there is likely much more to be had.

Also at Louisbourg walks the ghost of Captain Robert Duhaget. Duhaget served at Louisbourg and Port Toulouse (St. Peter's) and there are no records of his meeting an untimely death. However, he has been seen by many employees of the national park in the house that bears his name. He has been observed haunting the attic of Duhaget House in full French military dress, as well as walking along the grounds of the fortress, and even praying in the chapel each evening. No one know what he may be praying for, but one hopes he soon finds the absolution he seeks.

Scatarie Island

This large island once housed one of many small settlements that surrounded the French fortress of Louisbourg. After the last battle for Louisbourg when the British finally took complete possession of Nova Scotia, the French inhabitants of Scatarie Island were forced to leave. Today the residents of Scatarie Island report that perhaps not all the French have left. Some still remain, or at least their spirits do. There have been many reports of strange occurrences: ground shaking strangely; shadows that were taken to be the dead walking the island; gold buried deep with skeletons on top to scare away looters; ghosts of dead mariners appearing two days before their deaths; gold and more gold perhaps more gold was buried or lost here than anywhere else in Nova Scotia.

Sydney

Sydney coal mines

If you ask some of the locals around here, they may tell you some of the stories that abound about the coal mines and their ghosts.

One is about a coal mine that is abandoned now, but back in the days when it was a going concern, it was haunted by the spectre of a horse and a pit boy who used to work there. The horse was quite intelligent and was always paired with a young boy named Sol. One day they were killed when a tunnel roof collapsed on them. The next day an inspector claimed to have seen their ghosts working as usual, but his story was laughed off. Until the next day. Every day for a whole year at nine o'clock exactly, the same hour they died, the ghosts of Sol and the pit pony would carry out their duties as they did in life. After the year was up the spirits of Sol and his pony disappeared.

The Number 26 colliery was closed in the 1980s, but before that happened a forerunner saved the life of a man.

Other coal mines reported mysterious lights, some stationary, others moving as if attached to someone. No one was ever found though, and the lights may still shine through the lonely closed shafts to this day.

Whitney Pier

Whitney Pier has a haunted railroad story for you. Apparently the old roundhouse is haunted by an engineer who was killed there years ago.

Front Lake

This lake has the reputation of being a nice quiet place with a lovely beach. The lake itself is only a mile long and a half-mile wide, yet its peaceful surface hides a darker mystery, for in Front Lake there may be one of Nova Scotia's many sea serpents.

The first reports came from a family named Ferguson in 1820. They described a long, monstrous snake that was sleeping along the shore. Their appearance disturbed the creature, which promptly retreated into the water. There were no more reports of the creature until around the turn of this century when two men in a boat one night saw the creature in the middle of the lake. Another witness was on the shore and confirmed their story. Other reports have came down through the years of something strange and hideous sleeping on the sandy shore, so be careful if you decide to stop for a suntan or swim here.

Cranberry Lake

For more than a hundred years, nearby residents have reported seeing a creature living in the lake, similar to the monster in Loch Ness, with a horse-like head.

Barrachois

This is a rare occurrence in Nova Scotia — a ghostly train. The only other report of a similar spectre was somewhere in the Annapolis Valley. A phantom train glides along non-existent tracks along the St. Andrew's Channel towards the headlands of the Bras d'Or Lake.

Bras d'Or Lake

Local Mi'kmaq tell the legend of a lone phantom Indian who paddles his canoe up the lake just before a storm.

Victoria County

Bouladerie

The devil was cheated out of a soul one day and took his anger out on a nearby cliff. He heaved a boulder off of the cliff and threw it into a gulch, where it can still be seen today. Also strange lights are reported to have been seen flying over Bouladerie from time to time.

Kelly's Mountain

When the time came to put a new road through Kelly's Mountain it had to be built through land belonging to an Irishman named Kelly. Now Kelly was a drunkard and moonshiner to boot. He should have been happy when his land was appropriated for the Trans-Canada Highway; at least he would have had money for booze. But he was not, and he is apparently not happy even now that he is dead. The stretch of road as the highway descends to the Bras d'Or Bridge has seen more than its share of accidents. Some say that the ghost of Kelly is the cause of some of these accidents as he seeks revenge for being driven off his land.

Indian Brook

Somewhere between here and the North Shore are legends that Glooscap had a lodge in one of the caves that dot the shore opposite Bird Islands. This cave is also known as the Fairy Hole, and supposedly no one has ever reached the end of the cave. Some say these legends add further weight to the possibility that Henry Sinclair, Earl of Orkney, reached these shores, since we are pretty sure he reached Cape Breton.

Legend explains the presence of Bird Islands by saying that Glooscap was showing off for two maidens and, when he jumped from his canoe, he broke it in two and thus Bird Islands were born. The maidens were laughing at him and, being short-tempered, Glooscap turned them into stone. So if you want to search for the cave you must first find the two stones that guard the entrance to it.

Ingonish

Ingonish is home to a couple of legends. First, buried treasure supposedly rests in this area. Also, Keltic Lodge, a popular resort, is haunted. The ghost of Henry Clay Corson has haunted the lodge off and on since it was built in 1952. He came to this place at the turn of the century with the famous inventor, Alexander Graham Bell, who lived in Baddeck. Henry also liked the charms of rural Cape Breton and decided to make a home here.

Henry Clay Corson died, and in the 1930s the province expropriated the land from the rich industrialist's estate and built Keltic Lodge. Some employees feel he has returned to the resort. They have observed doors open and close on their own, televisions come on for no reason and, most hideously, a ghostly figure of someone from the knees down.

There have also been sightings of a smiling old man who mysteriously disappears after walking through the lobby.

There is also the story that some people saw the ghost of Mrs. Corson on the anniversary of her death. Two boys were walking along Middle Head, a narrow strip of land past Keltic Lodge. As they walked they saw an old man walking towards them. Soon he was obscured by some trees and when they next saw him he had changed into a she. Now there was an old woman walking towards them, with no sign of anyone else near. Soon even she disappeared, and the boys found later that it was the very same day that old Mrs. Corson died. It was then they realized they must have seen her spirit, perhaps taking a final walk around the place where she lived. But who was the first apparition the boys saw? Could it have been Mr. Corson?

Sugar Loaf

There is a fairy mound around here and if a brownie comes out and gives you some buttermilk, then you will be lucky the rest of your life.

Capstick

From Capstick along the shore to Meat Cove come reports of a hairy man-like creature, the second report of a Sasquatch-like entity in Nova Scotia (see Berwick). He is said to be more than eight feet tall, covered with hair, and have long arms that hang below the knees. An interesting difference from the usual Sasquatch sightings is that the creature's eyes are described as "beautiful." Hunters have reported seeing his tracks for years, and the last reports of the creature come from the early 1990s.

Inverness County

Margaree

There is a brook, called the Bochdan Brook, hereabouts that got its name from the wicked spirit, or Bochdan, that haunts the area. Apparently a drunkard died and was buried on an island in the brook and has chosen to terrify the living.

Margaree Island

Pirate treasure is widely believed to be buried somewhere along this shore. The only verifiable fact is that it is hidden across from Margaree Island.

Inverness

This area used to be called the Shean, which means "house of fairies." Many people have seen the little people and some refuse to walk alone at night.

Sight Point

Various animal manifestations haunt the area here, as well as a Bochdan (hobgoblin) that scares people and animals crossing over a bridge, a very secluded and lonely place.

Lake Ainslie

Lake Ainslie is a popular place for summer homes and cabins, but it is said that a sea serpent haunts it. Unlike most sightings of a sea monster, however, this one is described as looking like a whale with a couple of humps along its back.

Mull River

There is an apparition of a man with a slashed throat wearing a grey cloak, sometimes seen with a dog, who haunts the area and the Greve family. Apparently an ancestor murdered someone in Scotland and the ghost demands retribution.

Also, a powerful witch who used to keep locals in constant fright died at the age of 118 and her witch bag is buried in the vicinity.

Port Hood

Another famous phantom ship makes its "home" here, though it is seen throughout Nova Scotia and New Brunswick. It is the appearance of a sailing ship, fully ablaze, riding the swells of the sea. It floats across the water for a time, before suddenly plunging into the cold depths of the Northumberland Strait.

Antigonish County

Dagger Woods

Dagger Woods sounds to me like an area I would definitely not like to walk through on a dark and stormy night. Strange, awful cries come from the woods. The most famous Baucan (demon) of Nova Scotia supposedly haunts this area. It is said he calls to you if you walk along one of the lonely roads around here. There is a salt water spring in the neighbourhood that is haunted by the apparition of a grey clad man.

Caledonia Mills

From this lonely yet beautiful area comes one of the more well-known stories in Nova Scotia. It concerns a fire spirit that haunted one family, the McDonalds, in 1922. In some ways this story resembles that of Esther Cox, except there is no report of this phenomena afflicting one certain person in the house.

It began with floating balls of fire being seen in the house. Then small fires were noticed around the house. During one evening alone, over thirty-eight fires broke out in the house. Later, the phenomena included ghostly footsteps, pounding on walls, and unseen hands touching investigators who were called in. The family moved out for a few months, but upon their return the fires began again. There was also a strange animal sighted from time to time. It was described as a cross between a pig and a dog and was black as night.

Various explanations were advanced for the assorted phenomena, but none were entirely satisfactory. The age of the McDonald daughter was fifteen and teenagers are often believed to be the source of psychic phenomenon such as poltergeists, but this seemed to be much more. There was a theory advanced in recent years that the whole incident had been made up, since it resembled a case in England that had occurred just before it.

Lochaber

A story originates from here about one of the fairy mounds that dot the countryside. A woodcutter was on his way home to his wife and new baby when he accidentally stumbled into a mound one evening and partied with the resident leprechauns. He enjoyed himself for some time until an old man suddenly dragged him from the party and into the outdoors. It was then he learned the old man was his son and that he, the woodcutter, had been gone a long time.

Beech Hill

This hill has had strange goings-on for many years, all the way back to the last century when a pedlar got lost in the woods. Strange odours, a gray man with horrible features, and a Bochdan all inhabit the area.

Antigonish Harbour

In the woods surrounding the area, ghosts make nocturnal wanderings, searching for we know not what.

Malignant Cove

The cove got its name from the British warship *Malignant*, which was wrecked on its way to the battle on the Plains of Abraham. Although there is no official record of treasure being carried by the *Malignant*, popular legend has it that there must have been some gold aboard to help finance the campaign in Quebec. Lore has it the gold lies buried either in the wreck itself or along the shore. However, no sign has ever been found of it, or mention of the ship carrying treasure. Still, the belief is strong among the local inhabitants.

Pictou County

Merrigomish

Sightings have been made here of a sea monster that would also make itself quite nicely at home in a Scottish loch.

Melmerby Beach

Although not a ghost story, this next one is a mystery. It is here that in 1758 a man and his wife were brought over from England under armed guard. They were cared for by a group of retainers and the locals were told that the couple were members of the deposed Royal Family of England, the Stuarts. When the couple had a daughter, she was celebrated as the heir to the throne of England. She grew up and married, most locals recognizing her as royalty. She apparently got caught up in French intrigue and attempts to take over England and found her lands taken by the Crown. After losing her lands, she also lost her mind, levelling a curse on all who were against her. Local legend has it the curse was effective and if you feel like searching around the beach, you may find her grave tucked in the woods around it.

Pictou

In Laurel Hill Cemetery in Pictou lies the grave of a man who legend claims to have been a royal prince. On January 3, 1811, William A.H. Villers Mansel died and was buried in the cemetery. Although he never held a job, and was often drunk, he was always very well-dressed and had an endless supply of money. Apparently he was brought ashore from a British warship, and indeed, the capstone of his grave is said to have come from England. What is known is that in 1845 word was spread in England of the need for repairs on the tomb and Lady Jersey sent money to have the repairs done. Lady Jersey was one of the well-known mistresses of King George IV.

Pictou Harbour

In August 1803, a ship by the name of *Favourite*, out of Kircaldy, Scotland, unloaded passengers and freight. As soon as she laid empty she sank for no apparent reason. This led to considerable debate about the possible causes and after a while many locals settled for a supernatural one.

Apparently back in England, before the ship sailed, one of the passengers had a run-in with a witch. The man had shot at a suspicious animal near his cows with silver bullets, suspecting it may be a witch. He hit it but never found any body. He was never able to prove it had indeed been a witch, but an old woman in the town was suspected. She cursed him, declaring that he would never reach the New World. For this she was jailed until which time the *Favourite* reached Pictou. However, she was released early. He made it to the New World in time, but the ship wasn't as lucky.

Pictou Island

There is apparently a close connection between the "Phantom Ship of Northumberland Strait" and Pictou Island. The ghostly figure of a woman in white walks down a lonely road on the eastern side of the island to a point offshore where a bright, burning light awaits her. When the ghostly woman reaches the light it changes into the now famous sailing ship all aglow in flames. At this point the ship suddenly sinks, and everything is dark and quiet again.

Westville

There is a well-known house on the outskirts that is haunted by the apparition of a one-armed man. A polite question at the local Tim Hortons should elicit the location.

Epilogue

Many people have asked me why we have such a variety of spooks and specters in Nova Scotia. I think that, aside from the possibility that all these stories are true, it is our rich cultural heritage which gives us such a wealth of spine-tingling tales.

In studies on beliefs in the paranormal around the world, Canadians have been found to have the highest belief in all areas of the paranormal, especially ghosts and extra-sensory perception (forerunners, etc.). This is probably due to the diversity of our founding peoples. Not only the French and English, but also the German, Dutch, Ukranian, Irish, and others have such vivid folklore and legends in their home countries. They have brought that spirit of belief and custom to the New World, and new stories have grown out of that fertile ground.

In the eastern parts of Canada, the heritage of the founding groups is still strong and in some ways less diverse or spread-out as in the western provinces. In her book, *Folklore in Canada*, Edith Fowkes suggests that in British Columbia the three main strange stories are those of Sasquatch, Ogopogo, and Cadborasaurus, the latter two being "sea monsters." Although there are sea monster tales in the eastern provinces, our main staple of beliefs is built around traditional ghost stories, with buried treasure and ghost ships thrown in for good measure. There are only rare and highly unlikely stories of Sasquatch-like beings in the Maritimes.

My Uncle Al was a big strapping man with a keen interest in ghosts. He used to give me all his books on that subject, so I guess it's not surprising I developed a strong interest in the paranormal.

Once when my mother was visiting the family home, she asked Uncle Al if he often went upstairs. Uncle Al responded that he rarely went upstairs, for "there are too many ghosts up there!"

When my mother was twelve years old she was sleeping in the larger bedroom upstairs with my Aunt Phyllis. One night my mother woke up and watched a blue ball of light come into the room and float around until it reached the foot of her bed. At this point, my mother quite understandably hid herself under the covers, and the blue light vanished. It could have been a case of ball lightning, or it could have been a ghostly spirit revisiting its old home. Many people have died in this house, and perhaps some of them return.

Such stories often seem incredible or even impossible but there are clearly too many such examples to simply ignore.

If you know of any good stories to include in future editions of this book, or have something you wish to have investigated, please contact me at the address below and I will be pleased to talk with you. I am always interested in any story concerning the paranormal anywhere in the country.

Darryll Walsh
Center For Parapsychological Studies in Canada
6533 Edgewood Avenue
Halifax, Nova Scotia, Canada, B3L 2P1
Telephone: 902-453-1905
E-mail: novajodik@hfx.andara.com
Web site: http://members.xoom.com/novajodik

Appendix:
A short history of early
Nova Scotia

Although it has become widely accepted that the Norse visited Newfoundland a thousand years ago, the evidence of their visits to Nova Scotia is less certain, though quite possible. As well, there is growing evidence of the visit to Nova Scotia by Prince Henry Sinclair, Earl of Orkney, in 1398. This visit is someimes said to be connected with the Holy Grail saga. And of course, Aboriginal peoples have been in these parts for more than twenty thousand years.

The first European to officially visit these shores was John Cabot, Giovanni Caboto, an Italian, who ventured forth in the name of the British crown in 1497. Like many of his contemporaries, he was searching for the fabled

Northwest Passage, a shortcut for trade to Asia. He first landed on the mainland, then proceeded up the coast to explore Cape Breton Island.

After that quick and superficial visit, no other explorer visited these shores until Frenchman Jacques Cartier, who also explored Prince Edward Island and Quebec claiming these and the surrounding areas for the French crown.

This land dispute, though inevitable, did not cause any undue friction until 1613, when limited hostilities broke out between the French and English. Until that time, both sides concentrated on their own business and the land was large and diverse enough for both parties. The French named the land L'Acadie or Acadia and established the first fort in Nova Scotia, called Port Royal in 1605. It also came to be known as the Habitation.

Samuel de Champlain, the greatest French explorer in history, was meticulous in his charting of the region, except for two glaring exceptions — the first on the South Shore in the vicinity of Oak Island, the other on the Bay of Fundy at the Avon River — which may be related to the Holy Grail saga. He was also in charge of settling Acadia for the French, but he was not as successful in this endeavour as he was in his exploring.

After the destruction of Port Royal by the British in 1613, an uneasy state of affairs existed between the two parties until 1621 when Sir William Alexander was given possession of the land by the king of England. Sir William named it for his homeland, Scotland, calling it New Scotland or Nova Scotia. He began to settle the area for his king, but a treaty in 1632 gave all the territory to France. This was the first of many treaties between the enemies, with Nova Scotia the prize to be bandied about. France was only in possession of Nova Scotia until 1713, when the mainland was awarded to the British, but Cape Breton remained with the French. As well, Prince Edward Island and New Brunswick also stayed in French hands.

Upon the awarding of the mainland to England the French naturally began to feel a little threatened and they began to build up their defences in their territories. Forts and garrisons sprang up overnight throughout the area. On Cape Breton Island they garrisoned Fortress Louisbourg, now a national park and popular tourist attraction with historic re-creations of the time. At the time of its building though, it was one of the largest fortifications on the North American continent. Needless to say, this bothered the British who were trying to establish a toehold in the area.

In 1744, hostilities broke out between the two powerful rivals. After troops from Louisbourg attacked one of their settlements, the British laid siege to the magnificent fort and captured it in 1745. In 1749, the British established Halifax with four thousand colonists under Edward Cornwallis. The capital of Port Royal on the Fundy coast was abandoned and Halifax became the new seat of power. In 1755, the British seized Fort Beausejour on the present border between Nova Scotia and New Brunswick, and expelled all Acadian settlers in the region. The expulsion of the Acadians was later immortalized in Longfellow's poem *L'Evangeline*. Although some Acadians managed to come back over the years, most roamed far and wide, many eventually ending up in Louisiana, where their history and birthplace is found in the word "Cajun." The expulsion of the Acadians ended any major French presence in Nova Scotia, though it wasn't until eight years later that the Treaty of Paris formally ended French rule in Canada.

From that time on, a steady influx of British colonists changed the face of the province. But it is also important to remember the other groups of hardy settlers that helped develop the flavour of the province. Today there are large settlements to be found from the early Dutch and German settlers, the next two largest groups of immigrants. Sometimes we forget that although it may be more exciting to document the series of wars between the French and English, many other groups quietly went about the business of developing this province and forging a nation.

Once the wars were over, the people of this province were able to concentrate on day to day living and making something out of the resources of the land and sea. There were only two times that the integrity of the province was in danger. The first was during the American Revolution of the 1770s, when the upstart colonies looked northwards in our direction as part of a plan to defeat the British and create their own nation. The British firmly defended us from any encroachment, however, and it wasn't until the War of 1812 that we were again a gleam in the Americans' eyes. Again we managed to maintain our status quo. An interesting side issue is whether the Americans were defeated in the War of 1812, or merely held to a draw. They were unable to expand into Canada; the White House was burned by British troops, and most of the issues that began the war were unresolved at the end of it. Britain became worried more about her European neighbours and the United States grew bored of the war, so in 1815 both sides settled. It was mostly a useless war with nothing gained by either side.

Nova Scotia prospered during these two periods with the large influx of British ships and personnel on their way to battle. In 1848, Nova Scotia became the first self-governing colony in the whole British Empire. Nineteen years later, in 1867, the province joined with Upper Canada, Lower Canada, and New Brunswick to become the Dominion of Canada under the articles of Confederation drawn up at the Charlottetown and Quebec Conferences.

Bibliography

Baigent, Michael, Richard Leigh, and Henry Lincoln, *The Holy Blood and the Holy Grail*. London: Jonathan Cape, 1982.

Bauchman, Rosemary. *The Best of Helen Creighton*. Hantsport, Nova Scotia: Lancelot Press, 1988.

Bauchman, Rosemary. *Love is Stranger than Death*. Hantsport, Nova Scotia: Lancelot Press, 1985.

Bauchman, Rosemary. *Mysteries and Marvels*. Hantsport, Nova Scotia: Lancelot Press, 1991.

Bradley, Michael. *Holy Grail Across the Atlantic: The Secret History of Canadian Discovery and Exploration*. Willowdale, Ontario: Hounslow Press, 1988.

Broadbent, Terry, Editor. *Cries at Kinsac Corner and Other Legends*. Bedford, Nova Scotia: Self-published, date unknown.

Campbell, Lyall. *Sable Island: Fatal and Fertile Crescent.* Hantsport, Nova Scotia: Lancelot Press, 1990.

Caplan, Ronald. *Cape Breton Book of the Night: Tales of Tenderness and Terror.* Wreck Cove, Nova Scotia: Breton Books, 1991.

Columbo, John Robert. *Mysterious Canada: Strange Sights, Extraordinary Events, and Peculiar Places.* Toronto, Ontario: Doubleday, 1988.

Creighton, Helen. *Bluenose Ghosts.* Toronto, Ontario: McGraw-Hill Ryerson Ltd., 1957.

Creighton, Helen. *Bluenose Magic.* Hantsport, Nova Scotia: Lancelot Press, 1968.

Crooker, William S. *Oak Island Gold.* Halifax, Nova Scotia: Nimbus Publishing Ltd., 1993.

Crooker, William S. *The Oak Island Quest.* Hantsport, Nova Scotia: Lancelot Press, 1978.

Crooker, William S. *Tracking Treasure: In Search of East Coast Bounty.* Halifax, Nova Scotia: Nimbus Publishing, 1998.

Crowell, Bill. *Atlantic Treasure Troves.* Hantsport, Nova Scotia: Lancelot Press, 1985.

Evans, Millie and Mullen, Eric. *Oak Island, Nova Scotia: The World's Greatest Treasure Hunt.* Halifax, Nova Scotia: Four East Publications Ltd., 1984.

Finnan, Mark. *Oak Island Secrets.* Halifax, Nova Scotia: Formac Publishing, 1995.

Fowke, Edith. *Folklore of Canada.* Toronto, Ontario: McClelland & Stewart, 1976.

Furneaux, Rupert. *Money Pit: Mystery of Oak Island*. Toronto, Ontario: Totem Books, 1972.

Gesner, Claribel. *Cape Breton Vignettes*. Hantsport, Nova Scotia: Lancelot Press, 1974.

Henniger, Ted. *Scotian Spooks: Mystery and Violence*. Hantsport, Nova Scotia: Lancelot Press, 1978.

Jessome, Bill. *Maritime Mysteries and the Ghosts Who Surround Us*. Halifax, Nova Scotia: Nimbus Publishing, 1999.

LeVert, Suzanne. *Let's Discover Canada: Nova Scotia*. New York, New York: Chelsea House Publishers, 1992.

Mitcham, Allison. *Offshore Islands of Nova Scotia and New Brunswick*. Hantsport, Nova Scotia: Lancelot Press, 1992.

Mosher, Edith. *Haunted: Tales of the Unexplained*. Hantsport, Nova Scotia; Lancelot Press, 1982.

Mosher, Edith. *The Sea and the Supernatural*. Hantsport, Nova Scotia: Lancelot Press, 1991.

Raddall, Thomas. *Footsteps on Old Floors*. Porter's Lake, Nova Scotia: Pottersfield Press, 1992.

Samson, David Lloyd. *Island of Ghosts: Folklore and Strange Tales of the Supernatural from Cape Breton*. Hantsport, Nova Scotia: Lancelot Press, 1992.

Sherwood, Roland. *The Bride's Ship and Other Tales of the Unusual*. Hantsport, Nova Scotia: Lancelot Press, 1990.

Sherwood, Roland. *Legends, Oddities, and Facts of the Maritime Provinces*. Hantsport, Nova Scotia: Lancelot Press, 1984.

Sherwood, Roland. *Maritime Mysteries*. Hantsport, Nova Scotia: Lancelot Press, 1976.

Sherwood, Roland. *The Phantom Ship of Northumberland Strait and Other Mysteries of the Sea*. Hantsport, Nova Scotia: Lancelot Press, 1975.

Sherwood, Roland. *Sagas of the Land and Sea*. Hantsport, Nova Scotia: Lancelot Press, 1990.

Spicer, Stanley T. *Mary Celeste*. Hantsport, Nova Scotia: Lancelot Press, 1993.

Young, George. *Ancient Peoples and Modern Ghosts*. Queensland, Nova Scotia: George Young, 1987.

Young, George. *Ghosts in Nova Scotia*. Queensland, Nova Scotia: George Young, 1977.

The Author

Darryll Walsh, Ph.D., is a lecturer in parapsychology at the Nova Scotia Community College. He is also currently the executive director of the Center for Parapsychological Studies in Canada, a non-profit organization devoted to the scientific study of paranormal events and education of the public about these events. The Center takes a neutral look at all paranormal events and is interested in explanations, not dogma.